THE CONGREGATION

By
Robert Paul Durham

Edited by: Donald Wagner
Published: 2000

Copyright © 2000 by Robert Paul Durham

ISBN 0-7414-0544-X

Cover design by Cathi A. Wong
Published by:

PUBLISHING.COM

Infinity Publishing.com
519 West Lancaster Avenue
Haverford, PA 19041-1413
Info@buybooksontheweb.com
www.buybooksontheweb.com
Toll-free (877) BUY BOOK
Local Phone (610) 520-2500
Fax (610) 519-0261

Printed in the United States of America

Printed on Recycled Paper

Published November-2000

Author's Forward

There are four books in this short series and this first story, I knew, would produce the greatest challenge. For in the telling of this story, not only was I required to lay the groundwork for future books, but the story in this book had to entice you, the reader, to return to these characters, and more, in future books.

You may ask, "Where did these characters come from?" It's a fair question and deserves an honest answer, and so I will tell you. They come from life, my life and your life. Yes, your life. In fact, I suspect in your lifetime, you've met every

character portrayed here; and don't be surprised if you find yourself between these pages, and perhaps members of your own family. I didn't ask your permission to put you in this book, so I hope it's okay with you...if not...ce-lavie.

As you probably guessed, my son and some of his friends are here, along with other members of my family...and yours. I hope you enjoy meeting Jerrey and Terry, not to mention Gwen..."Wow!" and all the others, and don't forget to drop by Shelley's tomorrow morning for one of her delicious cinnamon rolls. By the way, have you seen a man in a dark brown overcoat with a red scarf wrapped around his neck? Shalom

Dedication

To all those souls whose paths have crossed mine
Family so dear and friends so fine
To small town living and big city dreaming
Precious moments that sweep by too fast, and precious
people whose friendship lasts
To sunny days gone by, and sunrise mornings
And memories of childhood joys and happiness
To right choices in major decisions
To cool night breezes, while swinging on the porch
And good conversations with neighbors
To special moments never forgotten along the way
And bonds made that shall never be broken
To life in beautiful places
And laughter that touches deep
To God who invited each of us into life
And has never left our side, never, not for a moment
I dedicate this book
Enjoy

Forward

Bob Durham has moved into territory that not many authors have traveled successfully. With this novel he has made writing that is Christian in nature, both entertaining, and creative. He has managed to do this while staying rooted in the simple "everyday" patterns of life that define individuals, families, and cultures. Who would have thought this could be exciting!

The way the reality of the church weaves its way through the lives of these people is at one and the same time serious, humorous, profoundly moving, and full of mystery...the mystery of God's grace. I even found myself here in this work, and that is the mark of good fiction, maybe you are there (here) also.

Bob has pulled off something special for Thanksgiving.

Albert F. Turnell
District Superintendent
North Georgia Conference
The Untied Methodist Church

iii

Preface

The first three days in the winter festival season fall during Thanksgiving. A national holiday in the United States, and elsewhere around the world, it is a time to remember all the blessings given to each of us in the midst of our life's many daily challenges. All too often our concentration is focused on the immediate need to solve the current crisis and, as such, all too often we miss the blessing giver...ever present.

Some see, and some don't. Those who do, have taken time to count. Take time.

Acknowledgments

To those few, who read this manuscript and gave their valuable advice; my thanks.

Table of Contents

Chapter One
DRUMSTICK SURPRISE

Thursday

They always gave him the turkey leg to eat. Not a whole one, mind you, but one that had been cut on till it looked like someone's chewed-on leftover. They called it a "drum stick"...and they always gave him some of that God awful red-purple cranberry stuff too.

"Don't forget to give Jerrey the drum stick," one of the women would say.

Like it was a big deal to get the darn thing. He had never asked for the dumb drum-turkey-stick in the first place, they had just always given it to him. Every since he was a little boy, they had given him the darn-dumb-turkey-drum-stick, or whatever you called it. He knew there were other parts to a turkey ("duh"), but darn if he knew what they tasted like. If they tasted like what they gave him to eat, they could keep the whole darn bird, far as he was concerned, 'cause he really didn't like turkey anyways.

He could never figure out why, every Thanksgiving, they had to have turkey in the first place. Why not some Southern Fried Chicken or baked ham? He'd settle for some "Buffalo wings", or ribs.

But n-o-o-o-, they'd have to spend hours in the kitchen, gibbering, gossiping and fixing turkey, then he'd have to eat that dumb chewed on turkey leg thing once again for another year. Lord, he dreaded the thought...dreaded it.

For now, he'd sit here in the Family Room with Dad and all the drive-in relatives, and watch some more football. At least that part of Thanksgiving, watching football, was good.

1

He hadn't made up his mind about all the drive-in relatives yet.

His older sister Janet Mae, a schoolteacher, and her husband Mark, a real estate attorney arrived last night with their two small children, displacing him from his bedroom and landing him on the couch once again for the night.

His older brother Bob, a computer, "whiz-would-be", had driven in from Cummings with Susan his schoolteacher wife, and their three brats, earlier that morning. Well, he shouldn't call them brats. They were okay kids. He just wasn't used to being around kids.

"The Underwriter" Christine, the sister right above him in years, just two years older than him, had just arrived not thirty minutes ago with her claims adjuster husband Todd, and their three "hooligan", boys. Well, he shouldn't call them hooligans but...well you know.

Back when Christine and Todd got married, Dad made a big deal out of Christine becoming an underwriter and marrying a claims adjuster. "Insurance, keep it in the family" Dad had said.

Big deal. Dad had spent thirty years climbing the corporate latter of a major insurance company just to get "downsized" at age fifty-five. "Downsized" was just another fancy name for kicking people out so you could hire younger and cheaper employees. "It was a cheap trick," he thought, played on devoted employees like his Dad had been "Downsize." He'd like to downsize a couple of Dad's old so-called, "friends" who still worked for the company. His Dad couldn't see it, but he could. His Dad's so-called friends helped "boot" his Dad out, so they could keep their jobs and protect their own rear ends.

But this was Thanksgiving. Dad, brother Bob, and brothers-in-law Todd and Mark, and he were all sitting in the Family room, sniffing that baked turkey and watching football. Mark and Todd were okay guys, he guessed. He really didn't know them that well. Well, after all, he only saw them twice a year, Turkey day and Christmas, sometimes. His big brother Bob was okay too, he guessed, but he didn't see Bob much anymore either.

Most of the time around here it was just he and Dad. Well, mom, but she was always doing something with other retired airline stewardess or attendants...or whatever they were called now. Fact of the matter was Dad still spent most of his days sending out resumes, and dreaming of "getting back in" again. God, he hoped his Dad would find something good by the first of the year. Maybe even better then what he had before. Maybe his Dad would get a job with a company that would buy his Dad's old company out, then his Dad could "Downsize" some of his old friends. It was possible! Wasn't it?

"Let's eat" his mother yelled from the dinning room. "Call the children in."

"Burt, Bob, Todd, Mark, Jerrey, come on. Turn that TV off and lets eat."

Janet Mae yelled, "Come on kids, lets eat," out the back door...and all the kids, with a whole lot of cold air, came rushing in through the kitchen door.

Everyone sort of moseyed around the dining room table, looking at the food and decorations...

"Burt, you're at the head of the table. Christine would you and...." and so it went.

He knew one day he'd have his own home and his own table and then maybe...just maybe he'd be able to sit at the dining room table with the other adults. But as for now, he knew where he'd wind up.

"Jerrey, if your have a seat right over here." His mother said, pointing to an attic chair brought down and cleaned up setting over in the corner behind one of the four covered-over card tables set up at the end of the room for the "children." The children! Here he was again, sitting with the children. Nineteen years old...nineteen years old, and still sitting with the "children!"

"Jerrey, help keep an eye on the kids if you will." his mother said. Now if that didn't beat all. Not only was he not old enough, mature enough, adult enough, good enough to eat at the dining room table, but he had just been appointed "baby sitter" for all their kids. Darn, he hated these holidays.

Walking over and around the "children" to get to his assigned chair and take his seat while others did the same, Jerrey Walker felt bad...or was it ashamed? ...or embarrassed?...or was it mad? He didn't know which it was or, if it was something else, he just knew he was getting tired of always being treated...last. Yes, that was it, last and maybe least in the family whenever they all got together.

With everyone seated now and the kids, "hushed up," by their moms, the family waited for Dad to give the traditional Thanksgiving prayer. Dad always gave the Thanksgiving prayer.

Jerrey, with his head bowed, waiting for the prayer along with the others, was still feeling, "least", or "last", when he heard his Dad say,

"Jerrey, would you give the Thanksgiving prayer this year?" What? Had he heard correctly?

Jerrey looked half way up towards his Dad, and saw that his Dad was looking right at him with a big grin on his face. His big brother Bob, with a frown on his face, was rotating his head between their Dad and Jerrey, and his two older sisters looked stunned...then looked at Jerrey. All the kids were looking at Jerrey, too. Everyone was looking at Jerrey. His Dad had always given the Thanksgiving prayer. It was a family tradition. But his Dad had just asked him to give the Thanksgiving prayer. Jerrey looked once more at his Dad, as though to make sure, and his Dad nodded towards him. Then Jerrey bowed his head again, and the others followed.

It was warm sitting there in the dinning room. The warmth reminded him of the girl he had noticed earlier that morning during a slippery, "Black Ice" ride downtown in his beautiful car. She had been standing all bundled up, but still shivering in the cold. She had been in line with the rest of her family. Her smaller brother, he guessed the little boy held in the arms of that woman standing beside her was her mother holding her younger brother, her father (standing there with that dark brown overcoat on and that bright red scarf

4

wrapped around his neck) had looked so familiar, but Jerrey had slide-driven by so fast.

That family had all been waiting for the doors to open at that big church downtown. That big church downtown was going to feed a lot of homeless people this year, he had heard on the TV. That girl waiting in line...she had been, he thought, about his age and so sitting in the warm dinning room, everyone waiting for Jerrey to offer this year's Thanksgiving prayer, a lump or something came up in Jerrey's throat and for some reason his eyes began to water.

"Cut it out", he told himself and opened his mouth to pray.

"Dear God, we thank you for this warm room to sit in. For all this food to eat, and this nice house to live in. For a warm place to sleep...and, and for all those who prepared it...ah, Amen"

"Good prayer, Jerrey," his Dad said, almost before Jerrey was through with it.

"Let's eat, I'm starved.   Boy you women sure out-did yourselves this year." his Dad added.

Everyone started passing food and talking at the same time.

The mothers handed "the children" their plates of food.

"Jerrey", his mother said, "I know what you like," and handed him a plate heaped high with food.

He might have known. There it was. As big as could be. A cut up and chewed-on turkey leg, big as your arm other food and, of course, a big glob of that God awful purple cranberry stuff.

"Thanks, Mom," he said with a forced smile. Well he had to say it. His mom was looking right at him when he looked up from the plate of food she had just handed him, so proud of herself for knowing what her son loved to eat at Thanksgiving.

"Wow, look at that bird!" Bob exclaimed

"Could someone pass the gravy?" someone asked.

"Where's the sweet potatoes?" asked another.

"Here have some of your mother's green beans," Dad said as he passed a huge bowl around the table.

And so it went, as they all ate and talked at the same time.

Jerrey ate the cut-up if not chewed on turkey leg...even that God awful purple cranberry stuff, like "a good little boy" ...plus much, too much more. Twenty minutes into the meal, and he was through.

"More, Jerrey?" someone asked.

"No, No thanks, I'm stuffed", he replied.

"Don't forget dessert, Jerrey," his mom said while passing someone the bowl of mashed potatoes.

Dessert, he thought, you've got to be kidding.

The kids finished first and ran from the covered over card tables, leaving food messes on both the tables and themselves. His niece Jocelyn spilled her milk on the covered over card table she was sitting at with Jerrey, and it ran, too fast, on to his lap. He jumped up and started to run upstairs to change his blue jeans, but discovered he had eaten too much to run...so he just walked fast.

He took his time upstairs changing. If he was lucky, he thought, all the desserts would be gone by the time he got back downstairs. Not that he didn't like desserts mind you, his mom and sisters made some mean desserts. It was just the thought of having to eat more that turned the dessert possibility into a reason to linger upstairs.

He must have stayed just long enough, because by the time he finally came back down stairs the women were clearing the tables, and the men were back in the family room yelling at the TV once again.

"Did you want some dessert Jerrey?" his older sister Christine asked when she saw him.

"No man, I'm stuffed!", he said again and eased towards the closet.

While no one was looking, he put on his heavy coat and hat slipped out the side door, and was just getting into his beautiful old Chevy, the one he had purchased at the junk yard last year and fixed up...when his Dad, walking towards the house with both arms full of wood for the Family Room fireplace, said,

"That was a good Thanksgiving prayer, son. I was proud of you."

Not knowing just how to respond to his Dad's compliment ...it was a compliment wasn't it? *Yes*, he thought...it was. Jerrey said,

"Thanks Dad" and closed the car door.

His Dad smiled and walked on towards the back door of the house, carrying the wood for the fireplace.

The old Chevy started with just one turn of the key. Jerrey slipped his beautiful car into gear, let off the brake, pressed on the gas pedal, and eased down the gravel driveway, onto the blacktop road that ran in front of his folk's house...and headed downtown. The heater in the Chevy worked beautifully, like the rest of his car. "Thank God" he thought. It was freezing outside. About the time the car got good and cozy, he had arrived at his destination downtown.

It was a big Church that was for sure. All the lights were on and cars were everywhere. But the line outside was gone. He sat there in his car, with the heater going at full blast, and the radio playing some Christmas carol...Christmas carol? This was Thanksgiving. Well, Christmas seemed to come earlier and earlier each year.

He almost drove away. But then he changed his mind and eased his beautiful Chevy into a parking place. After turning everything off, he got out and walked, "freezing", the thirty or forty feet into the lower level of the big church. It was warm inside like his house. It smelled like food. Good food like his house. There must have been three or four hundred people there, all eating their thanksgiving meal.

A lady came up to him and asked if he wanted to eat...

"Oh no thanks." he answered, "I've eaten already."

"Are you looking for someone in particular"? She asked.

He hesitated. He hadn't expected anyone to notice him. He wasn't sure what he was doing here in the first place except...

"I drove by earlier this morning", he said, "and saw a girl about my age with her mother and younger brother and father. They were standing in line outside. I guess they're gone by now," he said, even before really thinking.

"Well," the lady said, "I don't remember, but look around if you want. Sometimes they stay awhile, to keep out of the cold." Then she walked away and left him standing there, all alone and awkward feeling.

He could understand wanting to stay in out of the cold, that was for sure. But he didn't know if he should look for the small family or not. What was he going to say if he found them? Why was he looking for them in the first place? He wasn't sure, but he looked anyway. He was hoping he didn't look as confused as he felt.

The room was pretty quiet for so many people. But then again they hadn't come in out of the cold to socialize. They had come in to get warm and to eat.

He almost walked right by them. Almost right by, and out the door, when he saw them...right in front of him. He had stopped right in the middle of one of the many aisles to look, and there she was. The girl. About his age, eating, next to a little boy, her brother he guessed, and on the other side of her brother, an older woman, her mother he guessed. She looked up and saw him staring at her. Staring right at her. He didn't know what to do. There was an empty chair right there in front of him, so he grabbed it and sat down, across the table from the girl.

Just as he sat down one of the women who worked there brought him a plate heaped high with food. "Food?" What was he to do? He had just stuffed himself at home. There he sat in front of the girl and her family with a plate of food in front of him, and when he looked down he couldn't believe it. There on his plate was a cut up if not chewed-on turkey drumstick leg, and some of that God-awful purple cranberry stuff. For a split second he wondered if his mother had called ahead. But then he realized everyone in the big Church was eating the same thing.

He looked at the girl about his age and said,

"I drove by this morning and saw you standing in line with your folks and your brother, so I thought I'd come back down this afternoon to say hi."

8

How stupid that sounded, he thought. *Stupid! Stupid! Stupid!* He had said some dumb things in his life but that just won the prize. *How stupid!*

The girl didn't say anything, but her mother spoke up and said,

"That was nice of you to think about us."

After looking around he asked the girl,

"Where's your Dad? I don't see him?"

"My Dad?" she barked.

"My Dad! My Dad left us six months ago, said he couldn't take it anymore. That's why we're here. Mom and my brother and me, because of my precious Dad."

"But I saw your father. He was standing in line with you." Jerrey said.

"There are no men here," she said.

"They just feed women and children at this church. The men are fed across town at another church."

He looked around...and sure enough there were no men in the place. Just himself. He looked closer but the workers in the kitchen were all women, too. No men.

"There hasn't been any men around here all day," her mother broke in and said.

"But I saw him!" Jerrey persisted,

"When I drove by this morning he was standing in line with you three."

The girl just stared at him like he was some kind of a dope or something. Her little brother kept eating and her mother smiled, shook her head, and said,

"You're mistaken."

He felt like a fool. Like a darn full! Why had he mentioned her Dad in the first place? He hadn't driven down here to see either her Dad or her Mother. Why had he driven back down to the church? He really didn't know, but it wasn't to get her all upset about her imaginary Dad. Imaginary?

To change the subject, he asked where they would be staying for the night.

"We will be warm tonight," her mother said.

"We'll be staying here," The girl added.

As he looked around, he saw that some women volunteers were already putting out sleeping mats, and covering them with brown wool blankets.

He didn't know what to say. He was glad they would be warm...but he didn't know what to say. So he wished them well, excused himself, and scooted the chair out to stand up. As he stood her mother said,

"Thanks for thinking about us young man. What's your name?" she asked.

"Jerrey Walker ma'am", he answered.

"Well, you have a nice Thanksgiving Jerrey Walker...and God bless."

The girl wasn't eating anymore, but she didn't look up as he left.

He walked back out into the freezing cold to his car, started it, adjusted the heater to maximum, and drove away, puzzled, perplexed and wondering why? Why in the world had he driven back downtown? Why had he gone looking for the girl and why had he embarrassed himself so after finding her? Why? Stupid...was the only answer he could come up with...Stupid! Stupid! Stupid!

All the way home in his beautiful, warming Chevy, he wondered. He wondered about what he thought he had seen earlier that day. All those people standing in line...all those women and kids...but with them, with the girl and her mom and her little brother, there was a man. There was! And he looked familiar, somehow. There was!

By the time Jerrey arrived back home the women were making plans for who would sleep where and the men were still glued to the TV football games. The third game of the day was playing by then.

"Jerrey", his mother said, "you're on the Family Room couch tonight. Okay?" Like he had a choice or something.

"Sure, Mom" he answered, wondering when the last football game of the day would be over so he could get some shut-eye. Well, it wouldn't be for a while, he concluded after discovering it was only the beginning of the second quarter for the football game on TV at the time.

"How' bout a turkey sandwich, Jerrey?" his Dad asked.

"No thanks. I'm still stuffed from dinner, Dad." Still stuffed from dinner? Wonder what the family would say if they knew he had just returned from the big Church downtown, where he had eaten half a plate of food again. "Stuffed" was an understatement, to say the least.

So he sat in the Family room with the other men and pretended to be interested in the football game. While he watched the screen his mind went back downtown; to the morning line, to the girl and her mother and brother...to the man he saw standing with them in that dark brown overcoat with that bright red scarf around his neck.

Then he heard his Dad say,

"Jerrey, hit the couch, son." Jerrey looked around and discovered that he was alone in the Family room. The lights in the house had all been turned off except the occasional night-light here and there. He must have fallen asleep while thinking about the girl and her family.

He staggered from the chair to the couch, where his Mom had placed some sheets and blankets for him. He forgot the sheets, lay down on the couch and pulled one of the blankets, a wool one, up to his neck and closed his eyes. He looked at the clock on the wall: it was one thirty in the morning. He tried to go to sleep, but to no avail.

He thought, wondered, worried, and in his mind walked through the entire episode again and again. Finally, he dozed off. But he tossed and turned. Tossed and turned. Tossed and turned.

Bolts of thought startle the mind. Like super electronic explosions, they can bring forward past experiences and flood us with knowledge, wiping our plates clean, surrounding us with wisdom and revelation.

Jerrey was trying to sleep through his bolts of thought, when out of the blue...suddenly, without warning, like a bolt of lightening, he sat straight up on the couch...then stood up in front of it. He was wringing wet. A cold sweat had covered his entire body and soaked the wool blanket through.

He knew! He knew!

He knew who the man was he saw standing with the girl and her family!

He knew...and he began to shiver...all over...all over...all over!

Chapter Two
STANDING IN LINE

Katherine hadn't planned on standing in line in the freezing cold. In fact she hadn't planned on any of this. Standing in line in front of a food kitchen had been the furthest thing from her mind. If someone would have told her last Thanksgiving that this Thanksgiving she'd be standing in line with her two children in front of a food kitchen, well, she wouldn't believed them for a second.

Last Thanksgiving had been warm and wonderful with their small family: Bill, Ashley, Sammy and her. A wonderful Thanksgiving, she had thought. But this Thanksgiving...well, it had all happened so fast. So fast!

Married for fifteen years. Fifteen years...down the tubes apparently.

"You can move up some," a man's voice said. So she took a few steps forward in line, her fifteen-year-old daughter, Ashley, scooting their three suitcases along with them. Katherine had just picked up her three-year-old son, Sammy, again. He was cold and tired, and hungry, like everyone else in line.

She had met Bill just six months before they were married. It had been such a beautiful wedding. The first two years had been the roughest. Well, the roughest up until six months ago. Nine months ago Bill lost everything. Everything! It all started with a business venture that couldn't fail. You read in the paper, see on TV and hear on the radio about other people doing crazy things and losing everything. You think, *It can't happen to us.* Oh, Bill...Oh Bill.

"You can scoot up closer to the door now," the man's voice said...and so they did.

13

It wasn't just losing everything. Other people have lost everything and survived. Other marriages have suffered greater catastrophes and survived. Other...

It was just that Bill couldn't forgive himself. Couldn't. She had tried to reassure him. Tried to cuddle up to him at night and let him know it would be okay. Tried to encourage him, as he looked for a job, any job. She told him it would be all right. Other families have survived worse. Even after the bank foreclosed on their home and they had to move out, and into a small apartment, she tried to reassure him.

"Bill, this could be a blessing in disguise," she had said.

"Let's plan on staying here for two, maybe three years. Then we'll be in an excellent financial condition, and we'll buy another house. The kids will meet other kids and this will work out...it will be okay, Bill."

He had agreed. But failing at anything had hit Bill like a brick wall...like a brick wall.

Bill had never failed at anything before. His had been a life of one win after the other. Everything that Bill had ever tried before had worked. He told her he had messed around in high school but, in college, when he decided to "put his brain to work," then his grades had soared. His first position with a small corporation and Bill was the "Man of the Month" in no time. "Employee of the Month" ,"Rookie of the Year"...those were Bill's middle names.

His 'ego wall' at the office was covered with certificates and plaques. Bill couldn't fail. Or so they both felt. That's why she had gone along with him when he said he needed to take out a second mortgage on their home. Why not? Bill knew what he was doing. Bill was a "success man" from the beginning. But the Broadway adventure turned into a slide down "Failure Alley", for the entire family, especially for Bill.

She knew that failure could be devastating to some men. Even the thought of it failing, kept most from risking success. It had been devastating to Bill.

After the failure, for six months, Bill had taken one job after the other and lost them, one by one. She knew why. He was always thinking about what went wrong. What went wrong? Always blaming himself.

Then one night he didn't come home...and she knew he may never...oh, Bill...oh, Bill.

Katherine had done the best she could. All the city, county, and state aid for children and government aid for her had kept them afloat. Provided a place to stay and food on the table.

Then she got this hair-brained idea to move to a new town, new scenery, and new school for the kids. All new! It might help ride her of the bad memories. Though for almost fifteen years her memories were wonderful, the last six months...every since Bill had left them...those memories she wanted to leave behind.

All the agencies had assured her there would be, "no problem," with the aid money. But there had been. She might have known with the government running.... well, by Monday...after the Thanksgiving holiday, she would get it straightened out. Find them a small apartment somewhere in this small town, and start a new life. "A new life." That sounded good to Katherine.

"You can go in now," the man's voice said.

And so they did.

It was warm in the Church fellowship hall. Warm...with the smell of Turkey baking. The memories of last year, and the family, and the emotions came rushing forward.

She put Sammy down quickly and unbuttoned his coat. And then...she couldn't help herself. She had held up for the sake of the children. Held it together so they could find some kind of strength in her. At least in her mind she thought that. She didn't know if that was right or not but she had done it anyway. Now the warmth of the room and the smell of food, what she had lost, what they had gone through, all came crushing down on her and tears shot out from her eyes "Oh, Bill, why did you leave us? Why?"

Ashley was sure her mother didn't know, that she had just said that out loud.

"Mom, cool it! People are looking at us"

"I'm sorry."

Just then a gray haired lady from the church said to them:

"There are three seats near the end of that table over there. Why don't you grab them."

"Thank you," both Katherine and Ashley said together, and headed for the seats with Sammy.

As they sat down, putting Sammy between them, Ashley looked over at her Mother and said,

"Monday Mom. Monday, and we'll get an apartment and you and I will decorate it, and make it home." And tears filled both their eyes.

"You're right Ashley. It will be all right."

Just then, one of the women came up to them and asked:

"Do you know where you're staying tonight?"

"No, No we don't...not just yet." Katherine answered.

"Well," she said. "I know...You're staying right here. After you finish eating, come over there in that corner and see me. I have room for you to stay here tonight. No need to go back out in that cold. And by the way, the food is really good this Thanksgiving. Don't forget now."

"No ma'am, we won't forget. We'll be right over after we get through here.

"Take your time now. Enjoy your meal."

Two ladies placed plates in front of Katherine and Ashley then asked,

"Does your son like this kind of food or do you think he might like a cheeseburger and some French fries, or something like that?"

"Oh," Katherine said, "He can eat this. I wouldn't want--"

"Nonsense, there's no trouble in fixin him a special plate. Young man, would you like a cheeseburger and some French fries?" Sammy smiled and shook his head yes. "And a coke?" A BIG nod again. "I'll be right back," and off she went towards the kitchen.

"These people are so nice," Katherine said.

16

But Ashley wasn't listening, she was thinking. Thinking about last Thanksgiving and, and her Dad, all the years with him. She had loved her Dad. Adored him, would probably be more accurate. But then he had just disappeared. Left them...left her Mom, after all those years of marriage. Her Mom had gone through hell...just because of him. Too hell with her Dad! The son of a bitch!

Katherine and Ashley had been eating slowly, giving Sammy bites of their plates, when the woman came back with Sammy's cheeseburger and French fries. There was enough food on his plate to kill a horse.

Matter of fact, even though they had been eating and giving Sammy bites from their plates, there was still enough food on their plates to kill another horse. Katherine and Ashley, without saying a word to each other forced themselves to eat slowly...slowly. It seemed to soothe away the tension of the day. Let it go. Let it go and enjoy the meal. They didn't have to worry about the night and where they would be staying. Someone must be looking over them, somewhere.

The food on their plates was just about gone, when a young man sat down across the table from Ashley. Before he left, they would find out his name was Jerrey Walker.

Chapter Three
VERANDAH LOVE

The Habershams lived across town from the Walkers. In fact they didn't live in town at all, but three miles outside of the city limits on a two hundred and sixty acre horse ranch. Well, it had been a horse ranch for years, when Grandpa was around, but he hadn't been around for decades now.

Grandpa Habersham had purchased the land from Tommy Smith back at the turn of the century. Tommy had inherited it from his father. But since Tommy didn't want to live on the ranch he sold it at a bargain price to Grandpa, and Grandpa had turned it into a gold mine. He bred, trained, housed, and sold horses for most of the residence in the county. But Grandpa had left one day, and had never returned.

The Habershams were Church members. And like many southern families who were members of a Church, every Sunday morning, well, most Sunday mornings, the entire family would get up, and go to worship. They would sit, stand, sing, listen, pray, pay and leave together as a family. Their favorite hymn was, "Standing on the promises." It had been Grandpa's favorite. They would even pray as a family during the week, over meals, of course. But there were those times when the entire family could hear Grandma Habersham in her and Grandpa's bedroom, praying. They always knew when she was through. She would always end her prayer by saying, "Thank you, Jesus. Thank you, Jesus." Sometimes her prayers were so long and so loud that, when she finished, others in the family through out the house would say with her, "Thank you, Jesus. Thank you Jesus."

Each afternoon, seven days a week, late in the afternoon, the entire family would migrate to the second floor verandah.

Like a magnet, wherever ever they were, whatever they were doing...late in the afternoon the entire family would migrate to the second floor verandah. It was a tradition Grandpa had started decades earlier.

Usually Grandma would arrive first. She felt it was her job to make sure everything was in order before the rest of the family arrived on the second floor verandah. There wasn't much for her to do. The family's maid, Mary, took care of most of it.

"Make sure all five of the rocking chairs are wiped off, Mary." Every day for decades she had given Mary the same instructions. The small circular wrought-iron table had to be covered with a white linen tablecloth, with a large bowl of mixed fruit sitting in the middle.

"Mary, don't forget the hot apple cider for my grandson, Terry. Coke in a glass with ice cubes to the top for my granddaughter, Gwen." Everyone knew when Gwen was around. You could smell her coming. Wherever she walked the entire place would smell of lilac. Her mother Evenly would ask,

"Gwen, have you taken a bath in that lilac again?"

"No," Terry would say, "She's drinking it now."

"Betsy, she's a doctor now you know Mary." Grandma would say. "She'll want pure ice water with a lemon slice in it Mary."

"Yes ma'am I know." Of course Mary knew Betsy the youngest granddaughter was a doctor. How could she ever forget? Grandma Habersham told her that every day...every bloomin' day.

"Evelyn, my son's wife, will enjoy sweet tea with me, Mary." Mary didn't know if Grandma Habersham liked Evelyn or not. Truth was she didn't think the old lady liked her daughter-in-law at all, but she tolerated her. After all, she was the wife of her only son. Her son, without question, was the spittin' image of his Daddy. Not only looked like him, but carried himself in the same manner: stately and elegant like.

Mary had been just a young girl when she was given the opportunity to leave the sharecropper fields her Daddy worked every day. Grandpa Habersham had invited Mary to be the "Main maid" of the Habersham Horse Ranch House.
Her Mama had said,
"Go ahead Mary, if you want. They're fine white people and they'll take good care of you. You'll have a better life with them."
It hadn't been like leaven home or anything like that. Mary's folks lived and worked a sharecropper farm just three miles from the Habersham Horse Ranch. She saw them often...when they were still alive. But they had both died years earlier and she had been at the Habersham's all these years. All these years, decades, every day, listening to Mrs. Habersham give her instructions on how to set up the verandah. Truth was, she kind of enjoyed the setten up time with the old lady. There was this long, long relationship between her and Mrs. Habersham. And when Mrs. Habersham's husband had gone on that trip and not returned, it broke Mrs. Habersham's heart...but it broke Mary's, too. They had both lost a great deal when they lost him.
"My son will want fresh brewed coffee, just like his Daddy"
"Yes ma'am, I know"
Mr. Habersham "Grandpa" everyone called him back then, and now, had to have his hot coffee "brewed from freshly ground coffee beans, thank you." Even during the heat of the summer. Even during August. Mr. Habersham, Grandpa, had to have his hot coffee, both women remembered. Grandpa had never smoked, never drank beer or liquor, but there was his coffee.
"Black, of course," he would say. "Why would you want to mess up a good cup of coffee with sugar and cream?"
And now the Habersham's son, Theodore- everyone called him Ted- was so much like his Daddy had been. Mrs. Habersham could see it...Mary could, too.

The tradition Grandpa had started years earlier had carried on. Late in the afternoon the entire family would migrate to the second floor verandah, sit in their rocking chairs, drink apple cider, sweet ice tea, coke, and coffee, eat fruit, talk, laugh, and watch the sun go down. It was the best time of the day, for all of them.

Like everyone else's days, some were good and some were bad. Sometimes everything seemed to fall right into place for each of them during the day. Other times nothing seemed to go right. It usually started in the morning, about the time they each left the house. Each could tell rather it was going to be a "good day" or "one of those days", early on...and true to their early predictions, that was usually the way the day turned out. Like the day Evelyn arrived at work and discovered she had forgotten her purse "with everything in it." The day Grandma stepped off the curb while shopping with Mary, and broke her ankle. She knew it was going to be one of those days. The day Terry was packing to leave on a weekend fishing trip with Jerrey Walker, and locked his keys in the trunk. The day Betsy went to her office, instead of the hospital where a woman was waiting to give birth. The day...on and on...you see, there were, "those days," but regardless, regardless...late in the afternoon, the entire family would migrate to the second floor verandah. There to drink refreshing drinks, nibble on sweet fruit, talk and laugh about the day's activities and watch the sun go down...and this Thanksgiving Day would be no exception.

Mary and Grandma had been working on the, "big Thanksgiving dinner" for days. Planning, buying, preparing...

"Is there anything I can do to help?" everyone asked.

"No, no," either Grandma or Mary would answer.

"We've got it all taken care of, thank you," one of them would add.

Each year as Thanksgiving drew closer, Grandma's and Mary's excitement carried over to the rest of the family and, by Thanksgiving day, the entire house would be filled with anticipation...and this Thanksgiving was no exception.

Ted had invited Bud Johnson, State Senator Bud Johnson, to, "share the day", with the family and Bud had graciously accepted. Bud was all alone now. Divorced you know. His wife had won custody of the children and had left, taking their three "young'uns", with her back to her parent's hometown where she had grown up, in Fairmont West Virginia. Lord, he missed them.

It was the first time Ted had asked anyone over for Thanksgiving, though his Daddy, Grandpa had done that often, both Mary and his mother remembered. Just like his Daddy, more and more everyday.

In fact, Ted was just walking by the front door when he heard the door chimes ring, and so he opened the door to see his guest standing there.

"Bud, come in, come in. Mama, Evelyn, Bud Johnson is here."

"Bud, its so good to see you again," Grandma said as she walked across the hallway's hardwood floors towards him, wiping her hands on her apron.

"Thank you for inviting me Mrs. Habersham," Bud said politely.

"Nonsense Ted invited you and we're delighted to have you with us today. Ted, where's your manners, get this man a cup of coffee or something. I've got to get back into the kitchen and check on Mary and things. Glad you're here Bud"

It was such a warm greeting from the old lady of the house that Bud flushed inside. He hadn't felt that welcome for months. It felt wonderful, and his broad smile helped to cover the moisture in his eyes.

Ted turned toward the Family Room and started to lead Bud in that direction, saying, "Come on Bud lets--" when he saw Evelyn, his wife, walking from the Family Room towards them, Say hi to Bud, hon."

"Hi Bud, good to see you," she said as she gave Bud a nice hug and truly Southern peck on the cheek with her fire engine-red lips.

"Come on in here and relax." She eased her arm under his and led Bud into the Family Room with Ted following.

"Coffee, Bud?"

"Sure,"...and so it went. The three of them enjoying each other's company as they drank coffee, talked about politics, the town, and anything else Ted and Evelyn could come up with to keep Bud's mind off of his family condition. They shared the morning. Thanksgiving morning.

Betsy had been at the hospital 'til about noon. Gwen and Terry had been horseback riding. They so seldom got the opportunity to do that anymore, but they all met in the Family Room just ten minuets before Grandma announced from the foyer:

"Thanksgiving dinner is served."

They didn't need coaxing. The smell of turkey in the oven with all the other delicious smells, had made them all hungry hours ago. All of them stood up at the same time and headed for the Dining Room.

"Mom, you and Mary have sure out done your selves this time. Look at that table, will you?"

"Oh, Ted be quiet. You're embarrassing me. Senator, will you honor us by sitting at that end of the table and Ted will you sit at this end, up here?"

"Evelyn, if you sit right here..."and so Grandma seated everyone the way she and Mary had laid it out days earlier. While Grandma was busy giving seating instructions, Mary was standing over by the kitchen door thinking, *Spittin' image of his Daddy, Teddy is,...spittin image.*

They all ate too much. They said so. Well, aren't you suppose to eat too much at Thanksgiving? They didn't have the answer and besides, no one had nerve enough to ask the question. It was a delicious meal and they all told Grandma and Mary so. The two of them took the compliment gracefully, though they knew all along it would be coming.

Once the plates were cleared by the women and after a few minutes conversation around the table, the men rose and walked back into the Family Room, soon to be joined by the ladies. "Mar-e-ey," Grandma raised her voice,

"Come on in here and join us. Those dishes can wait."

In a few seconds Mary came in and joined the rest of the family. After all, she had been in the Habersham home for

23

many years now. She felt as though she was part of the family. Almost…almost part of the family.

Time flies when you're having a good time, and they were all having a good time talking and laughing when Mary said, "Mrs. Habersham, it's getting late in the afternoon and...."

"Oh, my word, it is," Grandma said as she got to her feet.

Both women left the family room and walked towards the back of the house, as those left behind continued talking.

"Bud, Terry here is thinking about entering politics. What da'ya think?" Ted asked

"I think he should keep on practicing law and stay away from politics." Bud answered.

"Besides, with him competing against me, I'd be sure to lose" Terry thought his Dad was losing it, and told him so. Politics? You've got to be kidding. Politics hadn't crossed his mind, not once. Wouldn't even consider it. Dad was losing it, that was for sure.

Everyone wanted to know what all was happening at the hospital, and so Betsy told them what she knew, which wasn't a whole lot. Doctors are the last to know, or so they say. Betsy played the game, but held back. There wasn't any reason to mess up everyone's Thanksgiving with all that was going on at the hospital. No reason at all.

"You know Evelyn," Ted said, "We'd better head towards the Verandah."

"The Verandah?" Bud asked.

"Yeah. Come on Bud, you haven't had enough to eat yet." Ted said as he rose, laughingy from his chair.

"Don't tell me we're going to eat again?" Bud asked.

"Hush now Bud, this is Grandma's and Mary's thing," Evelyn replied as she took his arm again and escorted him up the stairs to the second floor.

There was always a cooling breeze on the Verandah during the summer months when everything was open. You could smell the honeysuckle and dogwood, watch the tall grass blow in the wind, and catch the shiny flanks of a mare with her fold as they ran through the pasture. And during fall and the winter months, screens replaced with glass, it was always warm and cozy on the Verandah as the heat from the free standing fireplace and the warmth from one another's company surrounded each family member. It was the best time of the day, especially on Thanksgiving Day.

For it was a few weeks before Thanksgiving, decades earlier, when Mary, Grandma and little baby Teddy while sipping, eating, talking, laughing and enjoying the warmth on the Veranda, were told by Grandpa- halfway through one of his precious cups of coffee- that he had to go away on business for a few days. A few days? They had never missed an afternoon on the Verandah together since he had built this house. A day...a few days away?

"What kind of business?" Mary had asked before remembering her place.

"Horse business," Grandpa had replied.

"I'll be back by Thanksgiving," Grandpa had added.

And the conversation had ended with that. The next morning, Mrs. Habersham, with Teddy in her arms and Mary standing beside them, hugged, kissed, and waved good-by to Grandpa, sure they would see him by Thanksgiving. But Thanksgiving came that year and Grandpa didn't.

Mrs. Habersham and Mary called every hospital, police station, Sheriffs office, with in the State. No one had heard nor seen anything of Grandpa. For weeks both women called and called...but no Grandpa. The weeks, months and years went by. But every afternoon, late in the afternoon, Grandma and Mary would set up the Verandah, grind fresh coffee beans and brew a fresh cup of coffee for Grandpa. You never knew when he might just...show up. You never knew.

Mary and Grandma smelled lilac and knew the family was coming. When Ted stepped out onto the Verandah, Mary's heart skipped a beat. He was the spittin' image of his Daddy. The spittin' image.

"Here's your coffee, Mr. Habersham," Mary said, handing him a cup of freshly brewed coffee. Ted knew the effect his appearance had on Mary and his mother. He knew he was, "the spittin' image of his Daddy", as Mary was accustomed of saying. He even wore his Dad's cuff links and other jewelry his mother had given him. But he wasn't his Daddy, and never would be. He only hoped someday to measure up to half of what his Dad had been.

"Bud we're so glad to have you join us up here this afternoon."

"It's a beautiful view Mrs. Habersham, and it's been a beautiful day."

"Been? Well, it's not over Bud. Here, try this cool drink and tell me what you think."

And so he did. They spent the rest of Thanksgiving Day on the Verandah, talking, laughing, telling stories and watching the son go down. Just the way Grandpa would have wanted it. Bud never asked. He didn't have to. It was obvious. That freshly brewed cup of black coffee setting on the table, over to the side as though it was for someone special. Someone who had not arrived yet...and hadn't for decades.

Chapter four
SPECIAL FAMILIES

Karl Watts had been the Minister of the small suburban Methodist Church for two years now. The honeymoon relationship between the congregation and their Minister where the Minister can do no wrong, was over. Karl Watts was human, and the congregation knew and accepted it.

His wife, Alice, was truly an asset to him and his ministry. Not that she was present at all the church functions. Fact of the mater was, she wasn't always present every time the church doors were opened. But she supported her husband, and attended the Sunday Morning worship service on a regular basis.

That was all anyone in the congregation expected out of her. Karl and Alice had not been blessed with any children as of yet, but they were hoping and praying...and trying.

This Thanksgiving would have been the first Thanksgiving Karl and Alice shared without being with their families. Usually, in the past, they had gone up to her folks, or over to his for Thanksgiving; but this year things just hadn't worked out. Karl was wondering about the effectiveness of his ministry, and didn't want to have a heated discussion with his family over it; and Alice was recovering from a serious case of the "Crud", as everyone called it. Her nose was stopped up one minute and running the next. Her eyes were bloodshot and she felt like she had been ran over by a Tractor-Trailer. They had planned on staying home. That is, 'Ttil' Bill Junior. called and invited them over for Thanksgiving dinner. They were reluctant at first, until Bill Senior and Joy got on the phone and begged them to come. "It will mean so much to all of us," Joy had said.

27

And so Karl and Alice had accepted the invitation of the Bright family. They wouldn't be spending Thanksgiving alone after all.

Bill Junior and his folks were excited about having the Minister and his wife over for Thanksgiving dinner. They had really been a "godsend", to Bill Junior, inviting him into the Church and all. This Sunday, Bill Junior was to be baptized even. Ever since the date of his baptism had been confirmed, they had been on the phone inviting all their relative, friends, and neighbors to Worship this Sunday. They had even given serious consideration to sending out formal announcements, but wondered whom they would send them to, since they had already announced the event, by phone, to everyone they knew. For sure, this Sunday promised to be a "big one", at the Church's Sunday morning Worship service, at least for the Bright family.

Though the three of them were in different parts of the house, when the front door bell rang, Bill Junior made it to the front door first. Though by the time Bill Junior opened the front door, his parents, Bill Senior and Joy were standing right behind him, arriving just in time to great their guests.

"Karl, Alice, come in, Welcome." Bill Senior said.

Bill Senior, Joy, Karl, and Alice greeted each other then they all turned to Bill Junior...

"Bill Junior" Karl said.

"Sunday's the big day."

"Yep, sure is," Bill Junior. answered.

"I'm ready." He added.

"Come in to the living room. Dinner will be ready in just a little bit." Joy said.

"What can I do to help, Joy"? Alice asked as they all walked into the living room.

The two women walked through the living room, dropping the men off in front of the TV as they proceed into the kitchen.

Everyone knew to call Bill Junior, "Bill Junior" not Billy. And if you left off the "Junior" he would tell you so. His name was Bill Jr., and that was what he wanted to be called. Now, Bill Junior was a baseball player. He practiced all winter long for the upcoming season, outside when the weather was nice and on the inside when it wasn't so nice. Years earlier his father had purchased a baseball glove, a ball, and a bat for Bill Junior, and that was the start of it. From that moment on Bill Junior was a baseball player. If the weather permitted, he was outside throwing that ball up in the air and catching it as it came down…right there in the glove. Along the way, somehow, he had acquired an additional glove and if you happened to walk by he'd throw you the extra glove and say,

"Throw ball with me."

There wasn't any discussion about it. It didn't matter who you were or if you knew Bill Junior or not. You just put the glove on, and passed ball with Bill Junior, for a while, whether you wanted to or not.

If weather didn't permit his baseball practice outside, everyone in the house knew he was down in the basement throwing the ball up in the air and catching it when it came down. Everyone knew because, as the ball went up, it would hit the boards under the kitchen floor and make a thud. Not once, but every time he threw it up. Time after time after time.... Once in a while he would throw the ball against the wall, down there. Once in a while, but not enough.

When it came to batting practice Bill Junior's attitude was the same. Everyone who walked by was a potential pitcher. He'd say, "Throw me the ball, will you?" And most would accommodate Bill Jr. by winding up and pitching him the ball. Bill Jr. wasn't bad at playing baseball. Fact was, he was pretty good. When the day came for the "Big Game", Bill Jr. was ready.

Bill Jr. was up early the morning of the, "Big Game." He put on his baseball cap, picked up gloves, his bat, and both his baseballs, and headed towards the field, not knowing what excitement lay ahead.

One of his friends was chosen team captain. That made Bill Jr. relaxed a little. While he would never admit it, he had been a little worried about being picked to play. Standing in line, waiting to be picked, can be worrisome. He never liked that part. For some reason, he always felt as though he might be left out, not picked to play. He didn't know why he worried about it, he just did.

When his friend, the team captain, didn't pick Bill Junior to be the first player on the team, Bill Jr. started his worrying. The guy he picked was a good player, Bill Jr. knew. The second guy was picked, then the third and fourth. Bill Jr. really started worrying.

"Bill Junior" his friend called...

Well he didn't have to worry about it anymore, this time. Not this day. Not on the day of the "Big Game." He had just been chosen to play.

"Right field, Bill Junior," his friend ordered.

Bill Jr. joined the team and headed out to right field. As he ran out to his assigned position, Bill Junior stuffed first one, then two, and eventually three wads of bubble gum into this mouth. They wouldn't' let the players chew tobacco. Chewing tobacco wasn't good for you anyway. So they all chewed bubble gum. Well, most of them did. Bill Junior sure did. With three wads of bubble gum in his mouth, Bill Junior was ready to "play ball!" His jaw, full of bubble gum, stuck way out on one side. He could spit and blow a bubble, "Big as you're head, man."

Inning after inning they played baseball. It was a close game. It was the bottom of the ninth inning. The other side was up to bat and Bill Jr. was in right field, waiting...waiting. The bubble gum moved, front and center in his mouth. His tongue pushed out and Bill Jr. began to blow. At first it was just a normal bubble, then it got bigger and bigger. Soon it covered Bill Junior's face and eyes, he had to look down to see home plate.

Then he heard the sound of the bat hitting the ball. It was a loud crack. He knew it might be a home run. Bill Jr. looked up and the ball was headed right towards him. Right at him! The bubble continued to grow as Bill Junior exhaled in anticipation of the ball's arrival.

Something had to give. He couldn't take his eyes off the ball, he might lose it in the sun, and he knew that. So while keeping his eyes on the ball coming towards him, he whipped the huge monster bubble away from his face with his baseball glove, getting the bubble all over the inside of his glove, but he kept his eyes on the ball. The ball seemed to be hung up in the air, as though it might not come down. But Bill Junior finally saw that it was surely dropping, and right at him. This would be the play of the game he knew it. He couldn't blow it. He had to do it right. When the ball arrived, Bill Junior reached for it but his glove missed, and the ball hit him on top of the head…right on top of his head.

Stunned, shocked, not believing he had lost the ball in the sun and it had hit him right on top of the head, Bill Junior was just about to pause when he saw, out of the corner of his eye, the ball slowly falling to the ground. He reached down and caught the ball in his baseball glove right before it hit the ground.

The crowd roared. He could hear them. He knew he had to get the ball to the first baseman so Bill Junior reached into this baseball glove...and discovered that his monster bubble had surrounded the ball. With no time to spare, Bill Junior picked the baseball out of his baseball glove, bubble gum and all and threw it towards the first base. It hit the ground right before it got to first base, rolling in the dirt and picking up some right before it got to the first base man. The first base man picked up the ball and threw it to home plate. "Out!" the umpire cried. Bill Junior's team had won the game.

Everyone roared and applauded.

But the first and home plate players just looked at their hands, their gloves, and the baseball. Bill Junior's baseball.

The bubble gum, and dirt- covered baseball. It looked like someone had rolled it in some kind of crumbs just before cooking it. Its residue was everywhere. On his gloves, the plate...then everyone started to laugh at what had happened. They had all seen it. They laughed and laughed, everyone but Bill Junior

Bill Jr. was a little afraid to go in towards home plate to celebrate their victory with his teammates, as you can well imagine. He was a little embarrassed, to say the least. But, he finally had to head in. Embarrassed, a little afraid of what might happen to his baseball career-of what the guys would say, of what everyone might say or do- as Bill Junior headed in, he noticed the blond lady, the one who had been with him all day long, even watching him play baseball, come running up to him. She was laughing real hard as she gave Bill Jr. a great big hug and said,

"Boy, Bill Junior, you can really play baseball!"

Bill Junior said, "I can?"

Then he quickly changed it to, "I can!"

The coach came running over and said,

"Wow, Bill Junior, you saved the game!"

All his teammates came running up, laughing, shaking his hand and patting him on the back.

"Great catch, Bill Junior," one said.

"The bubble gum king!" said another

And so they celebrated: Bill Junior, the team, the coach, the blond haired lady and Bill Junior's parents who had shown up, just to watch Bill Junior play baseball.

Latter on that same afternoon, when it came time to hand out the awards, the announcer said;

"To Bill Bright, Junior. Best baseball player of the day...First place!"

Proud as anyone had ever been or would ever be, full of satisfaction and running over with joy, Bill Junior walked proudly over to the three steps sitting in front of the bleachers, climbed up to the very top step-the first place one- and accepted his "First Place" medallion in his county's,

Special Olympic Summer Games. And the bleachers came alive with applause...just for Bill Junior

Being a special, "Special Olympic" type of person wasn't Bill Junior's idea. He hadn't chosen to come into the world mentally handicapped, intellectually delayed, intellectually challenged, mentally retarded, or one of the other names he had heard people use in describing him. It hadn't been his idea, that's just the way he was. There were a lot of things Bill Jr. couldn't do. He couldn't read as well as most people. He couldn't drive a car. He couldn't think through a lot of things, and sometimes he got things all messed up in his head. But one thing Bill Jr. could do well, better then most even: he could play baseball.

Everyone wanted to see his medal and Bill Jr. was most accommodating. They ate, picnicked out and, later in the afternoon since his folks had to leave earlier, the coach volunteered to drive him home.

Later that afternoon, just as the coach stopped his car in front of Bill Junior's folk's home, right before the coach let Bill Jr. out of his car he said,

"Bill Junior, I'll be by about nine in the morning to pick you up, if you'll go to church with me."

Bill Jr. wasn't sure if it would be okay with his folks but he thought it would be. He hadn't been to church since he was a little boy. It might be fun to go. And so he said:

"Okay, I'll be ready Coach."

Bill Junior relayed the information to his folks, and while they hadn't seemed all that excited about the idea of Bill Junior going to church, since the coach was going to pick him up, they thought it was okay for him to go and said so. While they had never told Bill Junior, the last church they attended with him, they were asked not to come back with him again. That church didn't want "his type" in worship. They, of course, hadn't been to church since, over fourteen years now. They were afraid for Bill Junior. But then again it was the baseball coach's idea. Maybe it would work out for Bill Junior.

The next morning, about nine o'clock, just like he had said, the coach drove up out front. It looked to Bill Sr. and Joy as though the coach was going to get out of his car and come up to the house, but Bill Jr. was out the front door and down the walk before the coach could take three steps towards the house.

"Morning, coach. Ready!" Bill Junior exclaimed as he jumped into the front passenger seat.

"I'll take good care of him," the coach yelled up the walk to Bill Junior's parents. They just waved and shook their heads. They hoped so. They hoped so.

Bill junior remembered being in church before, but it was a very long time ago. When he and the coach walked in through the front doors of the church, there were several people there that said hello to them, and "Welcome" to Bill Junior. He didn't remembering that happening at the other church he had been to years earlier with his folks. Bill Junior looked at the Sanctuary and thought, "This is beautiful." He didn't say anything, but he followed the coach as they scooted into a pew and sat down.

Just as Bill Junior sat down beside the coach, he happened to look up towards the choir, and in the choir was that blond haired lady that had been with him most of the day yesterday. He nudged the coach and said,

"I know her."

The coach looked, and said back to Bill Junior,

"Yep, she was at the baseball game yesterday."

"She gave me a lot of hugs yesterday. I liked them"

"Yep," the coach said, "She gives pretty good hugs."

While Bill Junior was looking at her, she waved at him. He waved back.

He loved the worship service, every bit of it. When they stood to sing, the coach gave Bill Jr. a hymnal but Bill Junior nodded and said he couldn't sing. The coach whispered in Bill Junior's ear for him to listen to the women singing behind him. Bill Junior listened, and thought, "She can't sing worth a hoot." Then the coach nodded to the man singing on the other side of the coach. Bill Junior listened and thought,

"Good night, he can't sing either." So Bill Junior began to sing. He thought he could do every bit as good as they were doing, and he did.

He enjoyed putting his dollar in the offering plate, and noticed that was more than some others had put in. He enjoyed shaking hands with everybody as they all shook hands, and 'shared the peace.' When the preacher said, in the middle of his talk, "...all are children of God." Bill Jr. really liked that. He wondered if that meant him, too-if that meant he was a 'Child of God' too.

He asked the coach on the way back to his house,

"Does that mean I'm a child of God, too?"

"Sure does, Bill Junior. Your a child of God!" the coach answered.

Bill wasn't sure what it meant, but it made him feel good that he was one of God's children.

Bill Junior's folks were waiting for him and received the report from Bill Junior and the coach with much relief and excitement. The coach said he'd be back next Sunday to pick Bill Junior up, and invited his folks to come along. They politely declined the invitation but said Bill Jr. would be ready and waiting.

Week after week the coach picked Bill Junior up, and took him to Sunday morning Worship service at the little church on the edge of town. Every Sunday the coach would ask his folks to come with them. Every Sunday they politely declined. The memory of their last visit to a Church with Bill Jr. as a little boy still remained with them. Besides, they were somewhat afraid they might, "mess things up", for Bill Junior, somehow, by going with him and the coach.

Somehow the coach must have picked up on that because one Sunday morning after dropping Bill Junior off he asked if he might speak with them. Bill Junior had already gone upstairs to change his clothes anyway so they said,

"Of course, coach. Come in."

After everyone had a seat in the living room the coach said,

"You know, Bill Junior is a very special young man. God doesn't give special people like Bill Junior to anyone. You two must have caught God's eye somehow. You need to know that Bill Junior will be lighting the acolyte candles next Sunday. Why don't you think about it, and join us next Sunday? Bill Junior would be proud to have you at the Worship service with him. I'd be proud, too. In fact the entire congregation, I'm sure, would be proud to see you there."

Bill Junior's folks said they would think about it. Fact was, that's all they thought about during the next week. They talked about it several times.

Though Bill Junior's father, a Vietnam vet and a full professor at the local college, and his mother a public relations officer at the local high priced car dealership, were both intelligent and well educated people, somehow their thoughts had become confused over the years. To be present and see their son light the candles at a Worship service. Of course they would go. Of course.

The next Sunday they were waiting on the couch when he came to pick Bill Junior up. They suggested that Bill Junior ride to the Worship service with the coach and maybe ride back with them afterwards. The coach, excited that they were going to Worship with them, thought that was a great idea.

When Bill Sr. and Joy entered the Church building, they were greeted with bulletins, smiles, and handshakes. They thought none of the people greeting them knew who they were, and if they had known that they were Bill Junior's parents, wondered if the greetings would have been that magnificent.

In the middle of their wondering, the coach walked up with Bill Jr. and said to all the greeters and ushers and hand shakers:

"This is Bill Junior's parents...Bill Senior and Joy Bright."

And it all started over again. The handshakes, the smiles, the welcomes, and even a hug or two. Bill Senior and Joy were overcome with emotion.

Tears surfaced in their eyes but they managed to keep them in check. Ushered into the sanctuary, the beauty of the place and the warmth of the people filled both of them with warmth. Soon the coach left with Bill Junior to get ready, and the choir began to sing.

Bill Senior and Joy had not been in a Worship service for fourteen long years...fourteen long years. A void lived with for years, becomes part of you. The mind accepts the emptiness as normal and the void as part of the whole. But when that emptiness is surrounded by filling warmth, the type of warmth that seeps through self erected walls, then the void is filled like a cup to overflowing. Void is no more. There is only the overflowing. The music of the choir was just about ready to overflow their emotions when they saw their son, their son...their "special" son, Bill Junior, walking down the center isle of that small church, with a short white robe on, carrying one of the candles that would light the big candles sitting on the alter. Their son was an acolyte.

Their emotions, kept in check just moment earlier, burst loose and tears rolled down the cheeks of both Bill Senior and Joy Bright. Void was no more. There was only the overflowing cup of warmth. One of the ladies near turned around and smiled at both of them and said:

"You must be so proud of him."

"We are!" they both said together.

"We are!"

After the service, many came up to them and spoke. Bill Senior and Joy were so proud of Bill Junior, and told him so. As they were leaving the Pastor, Karl Watts, told both the Brights how proud he was of Bill Junior, how pleased to see them at Worship service, and said he would see them next Sunday. Before realizing it, they agreed to be at Worship the following Sunday. In fact they looked forward to Sundays, week after week, after that. Sundays were beautiful once again, as they had been before their experience at that other church with Bill Junior, when he was just a little boy.

Bill Sr. and Joy became involved with all the activities of the little church, and friends of sorts with the minister and his wife. They had been a god send to Bill Junior and, in fact, they had been a 'God send,' to them.

"Dinner time", Alice said...

Katherine felt safe in the big church. There were a lot of women and children staying there in the fellowship hall with them tonight, but there seemed to be more volunteer workers then those in need. There were plenty of inflatable mattresses and warm woolen blankets. Monday.... Monday. She just had to make it to Monday. Then she would get things straightened out.

As they were getting settled, she met a young woman by the name of Jill. Jill Smith. It was the same last name Katherine had used. Smith. Though Katherine and her children's last name was really Broden, she had chosen Smith on the spare of the moment. Smith could disappear after she got everything worked out, she had reasoned. Smith could be no more. Broden, once everything was worked out, could come back.

Jill Smith seemed like a very nice lady, though somewhat depressed. Well, who wasn't? How could you be in these circumstances and not be somewhat depressed? But Jill seemed a little more depressed then most. She said her husband was staying in the men's shelter across town. He was going to pick her up in the morning. Her and their two darling kids. Cutest kids. Well, at least she had a husband.

"Good night, everyone," someone said.

"Good night"

Chapter Five
SHOPPING AROUND

Friday

Katherine, Ashley and Sammy were up early Friday morning, like all the others spending the night in the Big Church downtown. Jill Smith, that was her name, Jill Smith, the young mother they had met last night while preparing to spend the night, was up earlier with her son Bradley. He was running a fever, and like most concerned mothers, she was worried.

Jill found one of the volunteers and they called a local doctor, who phoned in a prescription to the local drug store, the church picking up the cost of the prescription. "I tell you, some people are angels, that's for sure," Jill said. While she was thankful, she wasn't relieved much until Bradley's fever started to go down about an hour or so after he took the first dose of the medicine. By then it was just five thirty in the morning. By six, Jill's daughter Anna woke hungry and Katherine took Anna to stand in line with her and the kids.

"Tom should be here sometime soon. The men's shelter eats a little earlier, I think," Jill said.

Katherine wasn't sure she was saying that to assure herself or the two kids, maybe all three.

The volunteers working at the big church today were all from a small Methodist Church on the out- skits of town. Their pastor was a nice-looking, pleasant man who seemed to be interested in everyone at the shelter. At least he spoke to everyone, asking each if they had slept well and if they were warm enough. He seemed to be especially concerned about little Bradley Smith. Had the fever broken? Was he getting enough to drink? You had to watch these flu bugs,

39

they would dehydrate you very quickly, especially in children, he told Jill. Was this her husband?

When the Minister said something about her husband, Jill's eyes lit up as she turned to see Tom being escorted by one of the women volunteers down the line to where Jill and the family were standing. After she anxiously tucked her arm under Tom's, Jill said,

"Tom, this is Reverend. ...I'm sorry...."

"Karl Watts, Mr. Smith. We've taken good care of your family. Have you eaten?"

"Thank you, Reverend." Tom said as he stroked Anna's head.

"Have you eaten, Tom?" Karl repeated.

"No, I left early to get over here. But I'm not hungry anyway".

"Nonsense," said Karl.

"I know this shelter is for women and children only but there are exceptions and you're one."

Karl handed Tom a plate and moved on down the line speaking to this person and that one.

Jill introduced Tom to Katherine and her children as they stood in line, explaining their situation as she did.

"Monday," Katherine said. "Monday". And they all understood.

After breakfast Katherine, Ashley, and Sammy thanked everyone at the shelter, wished Jill and Tom much luck, and headed towards the downtown-shopping district. Why, they weren't quite sure. That's just where they were headed.

As Jill and Tom prepared to leave the shelter of the big church, Karl came over and stated his concern for Bradley.

"Why not stay here for awhile and give the medicine more time to work?"

It didn't take much coaching from the minister for them to agree.

"Why don't you bring the kids and let's go upstairs. There's a nursery and plenty of experienced mothers eager to help. Maybe one of two of them can watch the kids for awhile while we talk," Karl said.

Again, it didn't take much and they were all walking upstairs to the nursery where they left the kids in the hands of four loving mother types. As they walked by the doors into the Sanctuary, Tom and Jill stopped.

"Want to go in?" Karl asked.

Jill and Tom looked at each other and nodded without saying a word.

The three of them sat in one of the cushioned pews in the middle of the Sanctuary and were admiring the beauty of the place when Karl asked;

"Where you' all form"?

"Well," Tom said, "It's a long story."

"I've got time," Karl responded.

Jill spoke first.

Seems she was from a "Well-to-do" family raised on the plusher east side of the town. Her maiden name had been Samantha Jennifer Leesburg. Everyone called her "Jill" for short. She didn't know why. They could have called her, "Sam" or "Jenny" but for some reason most everyone called her, "Jill."

Jill, like most women, loved shopping. Putting this on and that. Trying this out, trying that out. Drop her off at a shopping center or mall, take her by that large Department store, give her the checkbook or a credit card-didn't matter, anybody's credit card-and turn her loose. She loved shopping. Her favorite tee shirt pictured a huge mall, with the words, "SHOP TILL YOU DROP", on both sides, front and back. Captain of the cheer leaders, member of "The National Honor Society", steady date of the football team's quarterback, she had even been the Homecoming Queen her senior year in high school...the belle of the ball.

She shopped around for colleges. Visited several with her parents. Chose a well-known southern Ivy League college to attend. She applied and was not only accepted, but also given a full academic scholarship, which paid for all her tuition for four years. Well, it would have paid for four years but while shopping around for a husband she had met

Tom. She said when she first saw Tom, she knew he was the one.

Tom was a good-looking senior with a mind and-a- half when he met Jill. Destined to be in the top three percent of his graduating class. His future in the business world would be guaranteed. And so he had asked Jill to marry him during her sophomore year. She had said yes, of course, and they had been married in the college chapel...two hundred and fifty guests. Jill always thought she could finish college later.

Tom's full name was Thomas Alexander Smith. Of course everyone had called him "Tom" for years. Tom's father had died in Vietnam. He never knew him. His mother had raised him and his three sisters as best she could. Working as secretary here, as clerk there. With the help of Social Security they had managed. He had worked during the summer during high school and while he wanted to give the money to his mother for her to use to help support the family, she had refused.

"You save that money for your college, Tommy," she had insisted, and so he had.

He applied at several colleges and was finally admitted to an old southern Ivy League college, mainly because he could play soccer, he was sure. ...the same college where Jill had just completed her first semester.

"And you know the rest about college," Tom said to Karl.

"What brought you, and here"? Karl asked.

It not only was the abruptness of the question, it was also the shock of sitting in this beautiful Sanctuary talking to this man that caused them both to inhale and look down.

"Forgive me," Karl said.

"It's really none of my business, but maybe I can help"

"I don't know if you can help or not Reverend. It's probably too late to help us, but our kids now..."

"It's never too late to help Tom...and it's never too late to hope"

Jill continued.

"Right after our honeymoon in the Smokey's, we moved to Atlanta. Tom had interviewed for an excellent position as a junior manager in a major corporation with its international home office in Atlanta before we were married, and they called him during our honeymoon. Tom worked so hard, "Jill said.

"His career soared, as did his paycheck."

Jill worked at one of the banks close to their new house in the small village just outside Atlanta, so she could be close to home. Three years and two children later, their lives were almost perfect. Jill went shopping at the mall whenever she wanted. Tom went shopping...at...the office...and he found what he was looking for. Her name was not important.

Jill, the ever-faithful wife and mother, never lnew that Tom was messing around on her. Going to bed with another woman. Sharing himself, then coming home to her.

She never knew. But who was she to judge? After all, she was as guilty as he was.

"And how is that?" Karl asked.

"Well," Jill hesitated,

"You don't have to," Tom said.

"I want to, Tom. What we say here stays here. Isn't that correct Reverend?"

"That is correct, Jill," Karl answered.

"Well.... I can't believe this is happening to us. To us!

One day while I was shopping in the grocery, a man, a nice-looking man helped me pick up some boxes I had accidentally knocked off the shelf...and he just introduced himself to me. I thought that was very gentlemanly of him. I thanked him and that was that. But the next time I went to the grocery, he was there again. We spoke and he said he was going to have a bite in the deli after shopping. Would I care to join him? At first I said no, but we kept bumping into each other in the isles and so when he asked the second time I thought, "What the heck, its just a sandwich together." After that, I think I arranged to be at the grocery the same time every week. Well, I did. And we became friends of sorts at first. We stopped eating lunch at the groceries deli and started going out to lunch...after our grocery shopping. One day, he knew Tom was going to be out of town for the week, he asked me out for dinner...and I went. The dinner...the wine...I don't know for sure but somehow we both wound up at his apartment, and well, you can piece it together...one night Reverend, just one night, and one time with him.

I stopped seeing him...stopped going to that grocery. Told him not to phone me. Just one time...but, that was one time too many. I hadn't seen him for over six months, when he phoned one night. He told me that he had just found out that he had AIDS, and that I had better get checked. I did. I have the virus and I gave it to Tom. We both test positive."

Jill began to weep as she leaned in to Tom. He held her close and kissed her on top of the head. Karl was at a-loss for words.

Sitting with them, in that beautiful Sanctuary, *the world can be such an ugly place,* he thought...*How many young couples? How many indiscretions? How many had "fooled around", and not been burn?. But these two beautiful people with futures so bright...and now their glass bubble had burst. Caught. Stung. There were always some who couldn't get away with anything. He didn't know what all they had gotten away with in the past, but this time...this time they had been caught. What guilt she must be carrying. What a burden to bear. What pressure must be pressing against her heart? How quickly they would jump at the chance to erase the past and start again. A fresh start...but AIDS! He hadn't kept up with the epidemic, but wasn't there better medicine now? Hadn't there been some progress on finding a cure? Right now, that wasn't the main concern. The main concern was giving these people some hope,* and Reverend Karl Watts could do that.

"Jill, Tom," Karl said.

"So you've made a serious mistake. And I don't have all the answers. But, I'd like to try and help...if that's okay with you."

Karl's words seem to touch the very souls of both Jill and Tom, and Karl could see it. They welcomed his invitation to help, as he knew they would.

Chapter six
THE SEARCH

The search began in Jerrey Walker's mind before he opened his eyes. All night long he thought about the man standing in line with the girl and her mom and brother.

What did that man's face look like again? How tall was he? What exactly did he have on? What was he looking at? Had he looked at Jerrey when he drove by?

At five thirty his alarm went off. It startled him so, he jumped out of bed forgetting why. Then he remembered. He had a six thirty tee off with Terry Habersham. Golf? Who wanted to play golf now? There was this man standing beside this girl and her. He had to find them, and maybe Terry could help. Jerrey ran upstairs, threw on his golf clothes, ran downstairs and into the garage, picked up his golf bag, threw it into the trunk of his beautiful car and headed towards the golf course. He'd get Terry to help him. They had to find them, the girl and her mother and....they had to...and quickly!

When he arrived at the golf course, Terry was already on the driving range, slicing balls, as usual, and yelling at himself for doing so. Why he never listened to the "Pro", Jerrey would never know. Money wasted on how many lessons now?

"Terry," he yelled, and Terry sliced another ball.

"See what you made me do!"

"I didn't make you do that. Listen, put that club away and listen. We have a problem."

"You make me slice another ball, BOY, and you'll have a problem."

"Seriously, listen."

"What's wrong?" Terry asked.

"Yesterday I saw this guy...man...standing in line with this girl, and her mom and little brother. They didn't see him, but I did."

"Doesn't surprise me. Looking at girls always made you see things. Remember...."

"Shut up, Terry. Listen. This was different. This man was standing right there with them and they didn't see him."

"You mean...he was that sneaky"?

"Ah...Ya...Yes, I guess that's what I mean. I mean, there was something weird about him. Strange even. Like he was there but wasn't."

"You want to explain that one?"

"I don't know how to...I stayed awake all night worrying about them...and that guy...man.
I think we need to find them."

"Are you out of your mind? I've already paid the fees for both of us to play eighteen holes.
There's the cart. Forget it. You see another girl you like...look at that one over there.
Maybe I'd better go and help her with her swing."

"Listen Terry, cut the crap. I'm worried about them."

"You've got to be kidding. Listen...let's play and then we'll talk about it. Maybe we'll go looking for them."

"Looking for them...that's what we need to do..." Jerrey said, and turned away. As he started walking away, Terry knew he wasn't going to his car to get his golf bag out of the trunk, but to leave.

"Jerrey!" Terry yelled, and everyone on the driving range turned to look at him...several golf balls sliced while others hooked...it looked like a billiards game in the sky.

"Sorry", Terry said, as he walked away from the driving range after Jerrey.

By the time he reached Jerrey's, "beautiful car" as Jerrey called the pile of polished junk, Terry was out of breath.

"Wait, Jerrey. Maybe I can get our money back, and...."

"Cheapskate...get in the car...Besides, you paid I didn't," Jerrey said, and began to back out of the parking space before Terry had hopped in completely.

"Are you possessed or something? Why do we have to find this one particular girl? Is she that good looking?" Terry asked.

"It's not just the girl. It's her mom and her brother and that.... that guy...that man."

"Boy, wait till they hear about this," Terry said, as they shot out of the parking lot.

"Where did you see them last?" Terry asked.

"Downtown...that's where we'll head."

Jerrey's beautiful car's fiberglass exhaust purred, roared, and backed down as he shifted gears, weaving between lanes, passing cars. Thank God all of the lights were green as they headed downtown. Terry was convinced Jerrey wouldn't have stopped one way or the other. In fact he had never seen all the lights turn green as they approached them. Must be a new synchronization of the lights or something, traffic flow and all that.

When they turned onto Fifth Street and headed for the big church, at the end of the street, Terry new their destination. Standing in line, that's what his buddy had meant, he saw them standing in a food line yesterday. By the time the thought registered Jerrey had come to a screeching halt, jumped out of the front seat, and was headed into the Church.

"Hey buddy, better take it easy on that beautiful car of yours," Terry yelled as he tried to catch up with Jerrey.

In through the fellowship hall doors Jerrey burst, Terry right behind him.

They glanced around quickly. Jerrey knew who he was looking for. Terry didn't have a clue. A girl and...

"Do you see them?" Terry asked.

"Not yet," Jerrey answered, as he walked slowly around the emptying fellowship hall.

"Can I help you?" One of the senior citizen women volunteers, with a frown on her face, asked.

"Ah, Ya. There was a girl and a women, her mother and her brother...the girl's brother I mean...and they were here for dinner last night."

48

"Yes," the volunteer answered.

"Well," Jerrey said,

"Are they still here?" he continued looking around.

"Oh, I don't know, young man. I wasn't here last night. We're just here for the day."

"Well, who would know?"

"Know what."

"Know if they're still here?"

"Oh, I don't know."

"Well, could we ask somebody?"

"Well, who would you like to ask?"

"LISTEN!"

Terry knew it was time to step in to this conversation before Jerrey really blew his stack.

"Is there anyone here, who was here last night? " Terry asked with a smile on his face.

"No, I don't believe so.", the volunteer answered.

"Do you keep a record of who eats here?" Terry went on.

"No, that would be an invasion of privacy. We would never do that, young man."

"Is the Pastor, minister, priest here?" Terry asked, still forcing himself to keep the smile on his face.

"Well, I don't know. But our" minister is here."

"Well, thank God for your Minister." Jerrey chimed in.

"Could we talk to him please?" Terry asked.

"Well, I was a school teacher for forty three years and I don' know if you "can" talk to our minister or not. But you "may" speak with him," the volunteer said, not knowing how close she was to Jerrey's anger.

"I'll be right back", and she walked away.

Jerrey was fit to be tied, and Terry was a little frustrated, to say the least. They both walked around the fellowship hall nodding to this woman and that one. Some of the women wondered who they were and what they wanted...they could tell by the expressions on the women's faces. Another volunteer came up to them and asked if she could help but they told her another lady was looking for the minister for them.

"Well", she said, "Our minister is not here, he's in California for the weekend."

Jerrey and Terry looked at each other in amazement. If someone would put this conversation in a book, no one would believe it. This was ridiculous. Just then, they heard the familiar voice of their favorite senior citizen volunteer.

"Boys, this is Rev. Karl Watts, our minister."

"Oh, I thought they were looking for "our" minister," said the woman they were just talking to.

"No, no I told them that I didn't think "your" minister was here but, "ours" was. Then I went to get him."

Karl could see the confusion and unbelief on the boy's faces and began to chuckle almost to himself but they could hear him.

"What can I do for you guys?" Karl asked.

"Ah...well. Well there was this woman and her daughter, and her son...the mother's son I mean, and they were in here last night eating. Well, I first saw them outside standing in line and then I went home and came back. I ate a plate of food.... there was this guy with them..."

"Oh no," Karl's volunteer jumped in, "You must have the wrong place...this is strictly a women and children's food shelter, and we abide by the rules religiously."

Both volunteers liked the, "religiously" part and thought it humorous that it had fit so snugly into the sentence.

Karl could see that the big church's volunteer and his member, were having some fun at the expense of these two you men. He didn't say anything but put his hands on each of the two young men's arms and led them away. When they were several feet away from the two comedians he said,

"I'm afraid they're right. This is a food kitchen for women and children only."

"I know," Jerrey answered

"But last night I came in here and spoke with them, and all that."

"Well, do you see them now?"

"No. I've looked. They're not here."

"I don't know what to tell you," Karl said with disappointment in his voice.

Just as Karl finished, the couple he had been with upstairs walked over. Karl had forgotten all about them. He had left them sitting in the Sanctuary when his member volunteer came into the Sanctuary and told them that she needed to see him.

"Are you looking for the Smiths?" Jill asked.

"I don't know," Jerrey answered

"A mother, with her daughter about your age, and a little boy about three?"

"Yes, that's them!"

"They left early this morning."

"Do you know where they went?" Terry asked, deciding to join the conversation.

"No, I'm afraid I don't.... wait...I think they were going to walk downtown. Yes, they were going to walk downtown to find a paper and look for an apartment. Yes, Katherine was determined to get an apartment Monday," Jill said with enthusiasm, mostly over the fact that she had remembered.

"Ah, thanks! Did she say where downtown?"

"No, just downtown."

"Thanks again," Jerrey said as he headed for the fellowship hall doors. He was almost

to the beautiful car by the time Terry caught up with him and jumped in.

"Need I ask where we are going, Sherlock?" Terry joked.

"Downtown, Watson...downtown," Jerrey responded.

The car...the beautiful car cruised along the streets of downtown, its occupants looking, staring, and searching.

Katherine and Ashley had to stop swinging Bradley between them as they walked downtown. The streets were already getting crowded. Friday after Thanksgiving must be the biggest shopping day everywhere, they thought. Shopping. Some day they would have enough money to go shopping again, and buy something. As for now, the only thing they both wanted to buy was a newspaper. A newspaper with

51

classified ads of apartments for rent. Monday...would be here soon.

As they walked along the sidewalk Ashley noticed that there was a stack of newspapers laying on the floor right inside "Shelley's Restaurant."

"Mom..." she said.

"I saw them Ashley. But if we go inside we'll have to order something to eat and...."

"Coffee? Do we have enough for coffee Mom?"

"Yes, of course, I guess we have enough for coffee and maybe a roll or something for Bradley. He didn't eat much last night," Katherine answered.

"He hasn't eaten much for a couple days now, Mom."

They swung Bradley around and walked into the restaurant's front doors. It was warm inside. The warmth felt good. They took a booth about half way down the long row and were taking off their coats when the waitress walked up.

"Is it getting any warmer out there?" He asked.

"I don't think so,." Katherine answered.

"What can I get for you folks this morning?"

"Coffee, please. Two cups, if that's okay?"

"...

And for the young man, a nice cup of cocoa?"

"Yes...and how much is a cup of cocoa?"

"Oh, cocoa for good looking boys like this one is on the house."

"Oh, thank you. Yes, cocoa for Bradley."

"Bradley, now that's a good name. I'll be right back," the waitress said as she walked away.

Ashley scooted out of the booth, walked over and picked up a newspaper, and returned. The two women searched the newspaper for the classifieds and found what they were looking for in the mess they had created on the booth's table top. "Apartments for rent." They were reading together when the waitress returned with two cups of coffee and a cup of Cocoa with whipped cream on top. After she sat the cups down and they thanked her she asked,

"Looking for an apartment?"

"Yes," Katherine answered.

"What part of town?"

"I'm afraid I'm...we're not that familiar with the town yet to know."

"Well, 'bout anywhere's okay. Good town. Lived here a long time now. Say, would ya'll try one of these and tell me what you think?" She handed them a large plate, with three of the biggest cinnamon rolls piled on it they had ever seen.

Katherine didn't know what to say but as she was thinking, Bradley reached over and pinched off a piece and began to eat it.

"Little fella knows what he likes doesn't he?" said the waitress with a big smile.

"Here," she said, reaching for three smaller plates. "Put one of those big ones on this and see how he does with it," The waitress said, handing Katherine one of the smaller plates.

Katherine did as instructed. Ashley took one along with her mother and the three of them ate the most delicious cinnamon roles they had ever eaten, and drank cup after cup of coffee.

"Refills are free," the waitress had assured them.

After circling several apartment possibilities the waitress came back over and said,

"Find a place?"

"Well, we don't know yet but it looks like there are several good possibilities here," Katherine responded.

"Got a job?" the waitress asked. After all now, Katherine thought. Isn't that getting a little personal? This waitress had treated them very nicely, to say the least, but her question was a little nosy. Reluctantly Katherine answered,

"Not yet. You see we just got into town...."

"That all you got with you? What you're carrying?" the waitress asked.

"Yes.

Aint much."

"Come with me a minute," the waitress ordered.

Katherine looked at Ashley. Bradley was so stuffed with cinnamon role that he was about to take a nap.

"It will be okay. Bring him along," the waitress said again as she walked away.

Katherine and Ashley scooted out of the bench and helped Bradley do the same. They didn't know what the waitress was up to but she walked through a curtain-covered door at the rear of the restaurant and started up a flight of stairs. It wasn't dark in the stairway but fear of the unknown was ever present with both Katherine and Ashley. When they reached the top of the stairs, the waitress unlocked a door and opened it. She walked into a nicely decorated living room.

"Aint much," the waitress said.

"But it was home to me and the kids for years. They're all grown now and I moved out to my own home last year. It has three bedrooms, bath, living room and kitchen. Table in the kitchen and all the furniture are included. Interested?"

Katherine was speechless.

Ashley spoke up and asked,

"How much? How much will the rent be?"

"Well, what's the paper say those apartments are renting for?"

"Three bedrooms, furnished.... I don't...." Ashley said as she thumbed through the newspaper, making a mess of it again.

"Five hundred dollars," she blurted out, knowing while she was saying the words she was lying. The cheapest apartment in the paper rented for seven hundred dollars and that was a two bedroom unfurnished flat. She waited.

"Well, okay, five hundred it is," The waitress said.

"Utilities?" Ashley was on a roll she thought. Why stop?

"Utilities included. They're on the same meter as the restaurant. I'd be difficult to separate them. Utilities included."

Hope leaped in Ashley's heart.... HOPE!

"And the deposit...?"

"Now what would I do with a deposit? No, no deposit."

"When can we...."

"Well, you're, here ain't ya?"

"You mean we can move in right now?"

"Looks to me if that's all ya got, you've moved in. Rents due first of each month, first month's free."

Katherine stood there with her mouth open. She couldn't believe what she had just heard. Ashley had just rented them an apartment from this waitress. No she was more then just a waitress. "God, thank you...thank you...thank you...."

When Katherine finally did manage to open her mouth she said,

"I...don't...." Tears swelled up in her eyes.

"You ever been a waitress before?" The waitress asked.

"No?....Well, if you want, you're one now. Five-fifty an hour and tips. It's slow now but in an hour or two it's going to really get busy."

"You mean.... now?"

"Well, what else did you have planned for today?" The waitress asked.

Katherine looked at Ashley and both women looked at each other with open mouths. Then they rushed towards one another and embraced and began to cry uncontrollably, What else, indeed. They had an apartment and Katherine had a job...what else indeed. There was a God. Had to be. Someone had to be looking after them. "Oh God.... thank you Thank you." ...and it wasn't even Monday!

Jerrey and Terry cruised the streets of downtown for over an hour. They stared at the growing crowed on the sidewalk and in the store windows. No luck. Not a sign of them anywhere. They were sitting at a traffic light when Terry said,

"Let's go in and see Gwen. Maybe she's seen them."

Jerrey wasn't that interested in seeing Terry's sister, Gwen. She always smelled like she had just taken a bath in lilac, and she was always putting her arms around him and stuff. Flirting. That's what it was, she was always flirting with him. He didn't know if she flirted with other guys or if they liked it or not. It made him feel uncomfortable. However, the possibility that Gwen might have seen the girl and her mother and brother out-weighed his resistance to the suggestion and he pulled the car over to the curb. After feeding the meter they walked across the street and into, "Gwen's Perfumery".

There she was, behind the counter, talking with a lady about her purchase. When she saw her brother and Jerrey come in, she winked at Jerrey. Terry turned to Jerrey and whispered, "Better watch out after sis. She'll have you over in the back corner kissin' on you, and you'll forget all about that other girl."

The thought of Gwen Habersham kissing him was enough to kill a maggot, Jerrey thought. It wasn't that she was ugly. Fact was, Gwen Habersham was beautiful. Her long brown hair had just enough wave in it. Her face was something to look at, that was for sure. Her clothing always perfect, and the way they fit her...it was just that Gwen had always been around. Always flirted with Jerrey whenever she saw him. Even when they were kids growing up, and Jerrey would go over to Terry's to play. Gwen would be there, and as soon as she learned how to flirt, she did. And it bothered Jerrey. Embarrassed him. That was it. He didn't know what to do when she flirted with him. It embarrassed him. He wished she wouldn't do that.

"Well, what's my little brother and this strong handsome man doing out and around today? What's you up to, Jerrey?"

Lord, here she was now, her arms around his neck and up against him. She smelled like a.... well, he didn't know exactly what but whatever. Wonder who created lilac anyway? Who ever it was should be shot.

"Jerrey's looking for a girl with a family," Terry said.

"Well, Jerrey, I'm a g-i-r-l...and if its a family you want....."

He could kill Terry Habersham right now. Right where he stood. That no good lousy bum. "You wait," his eyes said to Terry. When we get out of here....

"No Gwen...a y-o-u-n-g girl," Terry said.

"Aren't I young enough, Jerrey?"

He was sure of it now. He would kill Terry Habersham when they got out of here.

"Gwen, listen now," Terry said, faking seriousness.

"Jerrey is looking for a young girl with a family, and there's this man with them Jerrey can see, but they can't."

"Well, sneaky-peaky Jerrey," Gwen said, as she stood there up against him with her arms around his neck.

Terry walked away snickering as Gwen released Jerrey's neck and took his hand.

"Come over here, Jerrey. I have some men's cologne you're going to love."

She sprayed his arm before he could stop her.

"Smell that, Jerrey," Jerrey obeyed. It did smell pretty good. Then she reached up and sprayed his neck.

"Let me smell, Jerrey.....ummmmmm...smells delicious. I haven't seen any girls with families in here all day long. Are you serious? You are, aren't you? I'll keep an eye out for...a girl about your age, Jerrey, with...."

"With a little boy and their mother," Jerrey said

"I'll let you know if I see them."

The front door opened and two middle-aged women walked in. Gwen walked away from the two boys and greeted her customers.

As they left her perfumery, both turned to Gwen and mouthed:

"Thanks, Gwen".

she blew Jerrey a kiss and the two of them were back on the sidewalk.

"I'm gonna' kill you, Terry."

And they both laughed all the way back to the beautiful car.

Alice Watts looked at herself in the full-length mirror. She was pleased with what she saw. At thirty-seven she could still fit into most everything she had hanging in her closet. She reasoned that she had two choices, gain weight and have nothing to wear or maintain the same weight and be able to wear anything in the closet.

What she was wearing was certainly flattering. A suit with the skirt cut the right distance above the knee showed off just enough of her legs, not too much and not too little. The jacket to the suit was cut just perfect for her, and the scarf around her neck opened to follow the lines of the jacket color softened and highlighted her face. And it wasn't a bad face at that. At thirty-seven Alice could still turn a head or two, even if she was the minister's wife. She didn't want to keep her appearance for other men.

She did for Karl.

She wanted to look good for herself, of course, but most importantly for Karl. They had been married for fourteen years now. The best fourteen years of her life, that was for sure. Though they had not yet been successful at having children, God knew they were trying. While he seldom said anything about it, Alice knew Karl really wanted to have children. They both had been to doctors.

There wasn't anything physically wrong with either of them. It just hadn't happened yet. They both said it would, when God wanted it to, but they both wished God would hurry up. God knew they were doing their part, and often.

Pleased at the way she looked, Alice glanced at her watch. She had plenty of time, no need to hurry.

She checked the upstairs of the house to make sure everything was turned off before descending the stairs to the first floor. Once there, she checked the downstairs and put on her winter coat. You didn't have to wear winter clothes often down here, but for a few weeks every year you were forced to. This certainly was one of those winter weeks. It had gotten so cold over the last couple days that there'd been a problem with "black ice." She wouldn't drive in such weather, but the sun had been out all morning and the streets were dry. She wouldn't have any problem getting downtown to meet Betsy for lunch.

Betsy Habersham and Alice had become friends over the past six months since Karl had been appointed to the small Methodist church on the outskirts of town. There just seemed to be a connection there between the two, right from the start. In fact today was not something unusual, Betsy and Alice met at least twice a month for lunch downtown. It was the ideal place for them to meet. Betsy worked at the hospital on one side of town and lived on the other. She had to drive through town to get to either. Alice was downtown often for various reasons, and they both enjoyed those "sinfully" juicy cheeseburgers at "Shelley Restaurant". So at least twice a month they planned to sin. It wasn't unusual except for today. Betsy had phoned to tell her that the test results had come back.

Alice was worried. She hadn't said anything to Karl. Sometimes women don't tell their husbands everything. Sometimes, Alice reasoned, they don't need to know. Of course she would tell Karl eventually. She would have to, wouldn't she? So far she hadn't said anything to him. She was waiting for the results. Worried and bundled up against the cold, Alice stepped out of their home and walked towards the driveway and her car. She glanced back at their home just before getting into the car and smiled. Their home. It sounded good.

When Karl had been sent to the small church, he spoke to the church about allowing him and his wife to buy their own home instead of staying in the church's parsonage. It wasn't a unanimous vote, but the majority agreed that their new Minister should live in his own home if he wanted to. And so they had purchased the two-story traditional and furnished it slowly, just the way they had always dreamed they could. She loved her home. She loved her husband. She loved the.... well, everything. Except she was worried about what Betsy would say. What the report would say. What she would hear.

Bill Jr. looked good in the jacket, though it was a little tight here and there. The tailor assured Bill Sr. and Joy that the slight alteration could be completed by tomorrow.

"Need this jacket by tomorrow ?" The tailor asked Bill Jr. as he pinned the back.

"Ya, getting Baptized Sunday."

"Baptized! Well good for you. Where are you getting baptized?"

Bill Jr. looked puzzled at the tailor as he said,

"Church, where else?"

"Well, of course. I meant which church?" the tailor asked, as he smiled at Bill Junior's parents.

"The Methodist church," Bill Jr. answered.

"It's the Methodist church on the outskirts of town," Bill Sr. chimed in.

"Oh yeah, I know where that's at. Well, we'd better get this jacket right then, for such a big day."

"Yep," Bill Jr. said.

"What about slacks to go with it?" the tailor asked.

"Well yes, we'd better look at a pair of slacks too, don't you think Bill Junior?"

"Yep."

The four of them paraded over to the slacks section in the department store and picked out two pair of slacks that would go with the jacket his parents were about to purchase.

"Bill Junior, let's go find a tie and a nice white shirt for you to wear," his mother said.

As Joy and Bill Jr. walked over to yet another section looking for ties and shirts, Bill Sr. sat down in a chair to rest, and think.

Fourteen years ago both Joy and he had been hurt so badly when that church had asked them to take Bill Jr. to another church to worship. For fourteen years they had shoved that hurt down deep within themselves. The hurt of a mother whose son was rejected in a place where everyone is suppose to be accepted. Bill Sr. knew that Joy had blamed herself for years. Asking herself over and over, what had she done wrong? Was God punishing her? And then being rejected like that. He had tried to embrace and strengthen her but it hadn't worked. Joy had been hurt deeply for years, and while he didn't want to admit it, being the strong male type, Bill Sr. had been cut to the core. And now look at them...spending the morning buying Bill Jr. clothes for his Baptism Sunday. Bill Sr.'s eyes moistened as he sat in the chair waiting for his son and his wife to return with a tie, and nice white shirt.

Alice made sure the car was locked before feeding the meter and heading for the restaurant. As she walked along the sidewalk she looked in through the restaurant's wall of windows to see if Betsy had arrived yet. When she saw her they waved at each other as Alice continued towards the front door.

"Shelley's" always smelled wonderful. Though Alice had never had one, she had heard more then once about the cinnamon rolls that were served in the mornings, which left a lingering sweet smell through out the restaurant the rest of the day.

The restaurant was about half full already by the time Alice entered. Betsy was sitting in a booth about a third of the way down the row, a good view with plenty of light. Alice hated eating in the dark.

"Look at you," Betsy said. "Not bad for an old lady."

"Old yourself," Alice responded as she slid into the booth.

"You know, this place always smells so good," Alice said, changing the subject.

"Yes, it's those thousand calorie sweet rolls they serve here in the mornings. Ever have one?" Betsy questioned.

"No, have you?" Alice inquired.

"Yes!" Betsy said in an excited whisper. "Don't tell anyone...but they are delicious."

"May I help you?" the new waitress said as she opened her pad to write on.

"Yes. Do you know what you want Alice?"

"I'm not sure..."

"Why don't I just bring you what you want to drink first? That'll give you time to look at the menu," the new waitress with "Katherine" on her name tag said.

"Great idea...Katherine," Betsy said. "Ice water with a lemon for me, please,"

"I'll have the same...no, give me a glass of sweet tea please." Alice added.

"Yes ma'am," Katherine answered as she walked away with their drink order.

As the waitress walked away, Alice became physically nervous. She leaned over towards Betsy and with a smile on her face but fear in her heart, she asked,

"Well?"

Betsy heard the question and saw the hope and fear in Alice's eyes. So Betsy went stone-faced. It was one of her best qualities as a doctor. She could put on her stone, no-expression face in an instant, as she just had for Alice. And she could see that it had worked. Alice sat back in the booth slowly as she looked at Betsy's face. She interpreted Betsy's stone face expression as a negative. Bad news. Not what she wanted to hear.

But Betsy couldn't hold back any longer. She leaned over towards Alice, in her stone-face professional manner, and motioned for Alice to lean in so she could talk to her very privately. Just as Alice prepared for the bad news, Betsy said loud enough for half the restaurant to hear,

"YOUR PREG-NANT!"

"What?" Alice asked with alarm." What did you say...?"

"You want me to say it again. Louder? Should I stand up so everybody can hear?" Betsy started scooting out of the booth.

"No...no. Are you sure? I mean, I know your sure. But...YOU DIRTY DOG!" Alice said. "You had that no-expression face on and..... YOU DIRTY DOG!" And both women started laughing and batting towards each other across the table with their hands.

"I'm pregnant?"

"Yes, Alice, You're pregnant."

She couldn't help it. She couldn't stop them from slipping out of her eyes and running down her cheeks. Joy overflowed that way at times. And Alice Watts was overflowing with joy.

"Oh thank you, God," Alice whispered out loud as she dabbed her cheeks with a tissue.

"Well, you'd better thank Karl, too, you know. He had something to do with this."

"Oh of course, silly. I'm suppose to meet him at four this after noon....

Can I tell him?" I mean, it's okay"?

"Why wouldn't it be?" Betsy replied, having fun with Alice's excited confusion.

"Well....I've never been pregnant before."

Just then, the waitress came back with their drinks and sitting them on the table asked,

"Have you made up you minds yet?"

Betsy spoke first and, while gesturing towards Alice, asked.

"Did you hear she was pregnant?"

"Congratulations!" Katherine the waitress said.

"Thank you", Looking at Betsy, Alice asked,

"Are you going to tell everyone?"

"Well, why not?" The waitress asked, motioning towards the line of booths and tables in the restaurant. "Let me get everyone's attention..."

Alice grabbed Katherine's arm as Betsy started laughing so hard tears started rolling out of her eyes.

"You're as bad as she is," Alice said motioning towards Betsy with her head, and all three women laughed and giggled while Alice and Betsy both wiped their eyes with tissues.

Finally they gained their composure and ordered lunch. They had never looked at the menu. They knew what they would order before entering the restaurant.

"Two of Shelley's famous cheeseburger plates, please," Betsy said, and Katherine still smiling from ear to ear walked away from their booth to place the order.

Jerrey wanted to park the car and walk the busy streets.

"You know we're stalking them, don't you?" Terry asked.

"We're not stalking them, we're looking for them," Jerrey responded knowing his would not be the last word.

"No, we're stalking them," Terry went on. "Look man, we've been all over town three or four times now. They are not here. Forget it. Let's go see if we can get a tee-off time and play some golf. Come on!"

As they were cruising down Main Street one more time, Jerrey caught a glimpse of a dark brown overcoat and red scarf.

"LOOK!" cried Jerrey, as he wheeled the car over to the curb.

"THERE HE IS!"

"There who is?" Terry asked.

"The man," Jerrey said, as he stopped the car beside the curb.

"Where?" Terry strained to see.

"He was right there," Jerrey insisted, as he pointed across the street to the opposite corner.

"Well, where is he now Sherlock? One second you see this guy and the next second he's gone. What is he, a magician?"

"Let's go!" Jerrey yelled as he hopped out of the beautiful car.

"Wait!" Terry yelled after him as he ran to catch up.

Jerrey led the way as they walked, ran, and walked down the sidewalk and around the corner.

"OH!" was all Jerrey could say, as he rounded the corner and almost ran into Alice Watts and Betsy Habersham coming out of "Shelley's."

"Hi sis...Alice," Terry said as he came to a shocked stop and caught his breath.

"Well, are you two jogging today?" Betsy asked with a smirk on her face, "Or are you both chasing the same girl?"

"Funny," Terry responded. "Seems Jerrey here is having drive-by sightings."

"Oh?" Betsy questioned.

Betsy had a habit of saying, "Oh"? -in that questioning manner, like most doctors. She could just say, "Oh?" in the midst of a conversation and spark a half hour response. But Jerrey wasn't biting at her "Oh?" this time...No sir-ree.

"We have to go now," Jerrey said as he squeezed Terry's arm and dragged him away from the two women.

Jerrey held onto Terry's arm for half a block, not even realizing what he was doing, so intent was his mission to find 'the man', not until Terry said,

"They're going to think we're going with one another," did Jerrey realize he still had hold of Terry's arm, and released his grip.

"Thank you, dear," Terry said, rubbing the arm of his coat.

"He's gone...he's gone!" Jerrey said, waving his arms.

"I've been trying to tell you that all afternoon. Now let's go play some golf. What do you say, man?" Terry pleaded.

"I'm not in the mood for golf. I need to find him. I need to catch up with him," Jerrey said with earnest.

"Well, we've looked and looked, Jerrey, and we haven't found him," Terry said.

"Well, lets just keep looking then," Jerrey responded almost pleading.

"NO! No, no, no. NO! Listen to me. Put it to rest. If this guy is around, like you say he is, then we'll find him. It's only Friday. We have all day tomorrow to look...All day. Tomorrow, we'll find him.... tomorrow. We'll make a plan and we'll find him," Terry said, hoping that would persuade his friend to give up the hunt, for now at least.

"Right now, lets get away from it. It will give us time to thinks things through. Lets go and relax and play some golf," Terry continued his plea.

"Okay. But no more wisecracks. I did see him again," Jerrey bargained.

"I'm sure you did," Terry said, and held his next comment 'til they were back at the beautiful car and getting in. Then he looked over the top of the car from the passenger's side just as Jerrey was about to slide in behind the wheel and asked,

"Is he green?"

As the two young men ran, walked, ran, dragged away, Alice and Betsy walked on to their parked cars.

"You know those two may grow up and be real men some day," Betsy said. Alice just laughed.

"Karl...or should I say, 'Rev. Watts' has really turned out to be a real man." Betsy went on

"Shut up," Alice responded with a big smile on her face, as she playfully back-smacked Betsy's shoulder with her hand.

Chapter Seven
SKELETONS

Bud Johnson had planned on getting up early Friday morning, the day after Thanksgiving. He didn't know why or what for, he had just planned on doing that. But he didn't. He slept in. It was one o'clock in the afternoon before he staggered out of bed, and headed into the bathroom for a shower, still half asleep.

Thanksgiving at the Habershams had been the most enjoyable and relaxing day Bud had experienced in months, if not years. No, not years: last year had been a wonderful Thanksgiving with his family. Months, the best day in months. The Habershams were a wonderful group of people.

"Wake up, Bud," he thought, "Lets get it together"

Even after his shower, Bud was still walking around the empty house in a fog. Empty house. No one there but himself. After spending Thanksgiving Day with all the Habershams, the house seemed even emptier. He had just poured his first cup of coffee when the phone rang.

"Hi, Daddy."

"Hi, Snuggles. How you doing?"

"Great, Daddy. I miss you!"

"I miss you, too, honey."

"How's Mommy?"

"Okay...here she is..."

"Bud?"

"Yes.

"Did you go to the Habershams yesterday?"

"Yes."

"Good"

"How are your folks?"

"Mom's a little cranky as usual and Dads having a ball playing with the kids. I don't remember Dad spending that much time with me when I was growing up."

"Well, Grandfathers and kids, you know"

"Yeah, I guess."

"I miss you."

"You miss the kids."

"I miss the kids but I also miss you, Ann."

"I miss you, too, Bud. But I think this is best."

"I'm sorry, Ann."

"I'm sorry too Bud."

"What do you have to be sorry for, you didn't do anything wrong."

"Well, I'm not sure about that."

"Maybe we could talk some more about that...?"

"Maybe...but Johnny wants to say hello."

"Dad?"

"Johnny, how's Fairmont?"

"Fairmont's great, Dad. Grand Dad and me are going to a movie this afternoon, and we're
 going to a game, too. Are you coming here to see us?"

"Oh, I don't think so, son."

"Why not?"

"Well, its a long story and....."

"Love you, Dad. " "Bye."

"Bye, Johnny."

"He's gone Bud...running outside."

"Ann?
Maybe we can talk sometime soon about us..."

"I...I've to go now Bud. I'm glad you went to the Habershams yesterday."

"Love you, Ann."

"Bye-bye, Bud."

And the phone went dead. It wasn't until the phone started making that awful loud sound that he realized that he needed to hang it up. God, he missed his family.

All alone, Bud Johnson drank his lukewarm cup of coffee, not even caring to warm it up. That's what he felt like, lukewarm. Not hot nor cold, but lukewarm. God, he missed his family. What had he traded in, for his illustrious political career? What had he sacrificed, for a fleeting moment of satisfaction...that had not been that satisfying? What...?

Karl Watts had plans for this Friday afternoon. He had planned to meet Alice about four o'clock at the house and head downtown to the game. Karl liked to get there early and just hang-out, watch the players warm up, grab a couple hot dogs or cheeseburgers. Alice seemed to enjoy it as well.
But it didn't look like Karl was going to make it.
While he really wanted to get away and go on with his plans, he just couldn't. He couldn't leave them. He just couldn't walk away. They weren't
members of his church. No one knew them. Why couldn't he just offer to pray with them, give them God's blessing and leave? Alice would be waiting. She enjoyed the game as much as he did, he reasoned. Why not?
Because it wasn't in Karl to just walk away, not Karl. This couple needed help and while he didn't know how he was going to provide it, he was sure going to try.
First of all, Karl thought, he needed some questions answered. While he knew they both had AIDS-or tested positive with the virus-he should say, he didn't know why they were here at the Church's food shelter. Where were they from, here in town or from elsewhere? What about the kids, were they clean? Well, he shouldn't think that Were they okay-negative-or something like that? What were their plans? Obviously, or maybe not obviously, did they have any money? Maybe they did, maybe they didn't. Did they have a place to stay or go to?
It hit Karl like a load of bricks! He didn't know if there was a place for people with...if they tested positive-if there was a place for them to go and receive help, in town. He had been here for six months now, and he didn't know!

"What kind of a minister am I that I don't know," thought Karl. "What kind?"

After jumping on his own back for a couple of seconds Karl moved on with his list of questions. How could he help? And that was all he could think to ask. Pretty impressive list, his ego thought, and so with his ego and list in hand he walked back over to the couple sitting in the fellowship hall and sat down beside them. He didn't want this to sound like an inquisition so as they drank Cokes and tea he slipped his question in, one by one.

A conglomerate out of the northwest purchased Tom's company. Which in turn downsized him out. He had attempted and, in fact had gone on, several interviews. However, though no one would ever admit it, he felt that once they found out about his physical condition, job opportunities that apparently were there before, suddenly disappeared. Time and again this happened to him. Eventually, disappointed, mentally and physically drained, he attempted to secure any kind of work, anything, just to pay the bills...but with no such luck.

Jill kept her job for awhile but lost it because the bank closed. She had tried to secure another bank position but it seemed as though the word was out about their physical condition and no one, but no one, would hire them. They finally turned for help and received assistance from various government agencies, for awhile. But it was not enough to keep their home or even both their cars. They managed to keep one car, which had been paid off prior to all this trouble starting. For a while, that is. They sold it, eventually. They had to.

These people were really depressed, but at the same time there seemed to be a spark of hope between them. "Surely," Karl thought, the love between these two is still strong. "Look at the way they touch each other's shoulders and..." Karl's thoughts were interrupted by his own training and experience. Tragedy can draw people together. And when two people are still in love, as these two obviously were, and they both feel the guilt of mistakes...tragic...tragic.

Without a doubt, Karl knew they had forgiven each other...but he could also see that each had not forgiven themselves. Guilt is a heavy load to carry, especially when you know your actions will result in your eventual death. Not only the guilt of the act and it's aftermath, but the fear of God's wrath, that your foolishness and in this case also your unfaithfulness-has resulted in the taking of your own life. Guilt is a terrible load, and on top of all their personal guilt for past wrongs and the fear of the eternal, was the guilt of leaving their children behind. Who would care for their children? Who?

As he listened, Karl knew he could help, at least with the guilt.

He took them back upstairs and into the beautiful sanctuary where they had been earlier in the day, and led them slowly, as the three of them talked about the same things, to the front of the sanctuary. Stopping with them in front of the alter, Karl said:

"Lets have a seat right over here," as he walked to the front pew.

As the three of them sat down, Karl continued.

"You know, Tom, Jill,- life can really be a challenge at times. Human beings are not perfect. We all make mistakes. We all make mistakes. Sometimes,-well fortunately, most of the time-the mistakes we make are little ones and we can correct our own mistakes...most of the time. Sometimes, however, we all make those mistakes that cause us problems. Sometimes, serious problems. I'm sure if you two could turn the clock back..." Even as Karl said the words they both began to nod their heads...and Tom interrupted him and said, "Boy, Reverend if we could turn the clock back"...and Jill said, "If only." Karl continued,

"I know. But we know that can't happen. You both made a serious mistake, and you got caught. You're suffering for it. The doctors will help. Medicine, I understand, is getting better in this field. So who knows what the future will hold for both of you? But on the other hand, who knows what the future holds for me or, for that case, anybody else?

What I see between the two of you is a deep and abiding love. You both still love each other deeply."

As Karl spoke, Tom and Jill looked at each other and embraced with their eyes. Karl continued,
"What I also see is that you have forgiven each other for your past mistakes. That is so important and so wonderful on your part. To forgive another human being for something that human being has done to hurt you...is so gracious, kind and loving. It's a different and deeper kind of love. Deeper then loving a person. To forgive a person is such deep love, and you have forgiven each other. That, Jill and Tom, that is wonderful."
Jill and Tom sat close to each other holding hands as Karl continued.
"But there is a problem. A serious problem yet undisclosed. It's sort of a hidden problem. One we don't often talk about out loud. Its sometimes called, "The fear of God". Fear of God comes from our belief that God is a God of wrath. Some of that belief comes from The Old Testament, when God revealed His wrath against a nation or even in some instances human beings. Some-most-of our fear of God, comes from the dichotomy between the so-called secular world and the Church. The Church says, "do right" and you have eternal life. Do wrong and your go to Hell. Society says, "do what's fun, you only go around once." So we run from God when we do wrong, because we can't always "do right" and we just proved it to ourselves through the wrong we just did. Does that make sense?" Karl asked.
Both Jill and Tom nodded as they said, "Yes."
Karl continued.
"But God is not a God of wrath. God proved that to the world through Jesus Christ. God gave to the world for one reason...so that all the guilt of the wrong you and I have done in the past, even the wrong we've done yesterday, can be forgiven. Jesus said so, time and again in the scriptures. Listen to me. You have forgiven each other...now God wants you to know...God forgives you."
And that's all it took. Tom put his head down between his knees and began to cry like a baby. Jill leaned over his back and wept with her husband who she loved so much.

"Oh God, I'm so sorry," Jill said first...and Tom followed. Repentance, there it was.

Karl's eyes teared along with theirs as he silently thanked God for the privilege of bringing this lovely couple to God's forgiving grace. Now all that guilt could be taken off their backs. Karl couldn't help himself. He leaned over, placed one of his hands on Tom's back and the other on Jill's head and said,

"In the name of Jesus Christ, you are forgiven."

They talked for another hour or so. Before he left, Karl made arrangements for Tom and Jill to spend the night in the big church again and gave them directions and bus fare to a location close to his church. They agreed to meet there just after lunch tomorrow afternoon.

As Karl left the church, satisfied that he had made the right decision to stay and help Jill and Tom, a man in a dark brown overcoat with a bright red scarf wrapped around his neck, standing in the parking lot asked him the time. As Karl glanced at his watch the man asked,

"Is there a game tonight?"

Karl never looked up from his watch. He said,

"Yes there's a game tonight. It's four thirty." And then it dawned on him. If he hurried, and picked up Alice, they could still make it to the game.

Karl walked as fast as he could towards his car...never glancing back.

Bud Johnson sat at the kitchen table most of the afternoon, thinking. He thought about Ann and the kids for a while, then his thoughts migrated to his illustrious political career. He thought about what all he had done, just to get elected to political office. No doubt some people were in politics because that's all they knew. They had grown up in a politically active family with other members of the family holding office. No doubt there were those who got into politics out of a sense of duty and a personal commitment to the community.

72

But not Bud. Bud had gotten into politics for what politics could give to him: power, prestige, position, and all the other bells and whistles. He had climbed the ladder quickly-almost too quickly, for he and the family to adjust, and cope with his ever-changing career. Along the way he had bargained, traded and manipulated people time and again. Bargained away his integrity, ethics, his morals, and traded in his family, just for the privilege to be full- time liar and cheat.

He promised people things he knew he could never deliver just to get their vote and money, and said things he didn't really believe for the same reasons. When the religious right started gaining numbers, and he discovered they were more than willing to use those numbers to exert political power and influence, Bud became a right wing religious conservative.

A died-in-the wool Democrat at the time of his political conversion, he was in the midst of switching to the conservative Republican side when he was told to stay where he was. "One of them," he was told, "posing as a Democrat, was good strategy." So Bud became a right-wing boil on the left-wing's lower posterior. Good strategy, good strategy. The right wing could look across the isle and say, "Well, one of your very own, Bud Johnson agrees with us." And they had done just that several times over the years. It had given Bud notoriety and guaranteed his reelection for the last three terms. Bud had made, their 'list.'

At first, Bud not only thought it was a smart move on his part, and good strategy on theirs, but that in fact he was doing the right thing. The right wing stood for morals, ethics, integrity and good old-fashioned up front straightforward honesty. So did Bud! Or at least that's what he told himself and everyone else. Truth, once he became intimately involved with their views, he changed his mind and Bud really didn't like most of what the right wing believed in the first place.

He didn't believe it was any of the government's business how a person lived their lives, as long as they observed the law, and extended the same rights and privileges to everyone else. He didn't believe you could legislate morality, and frankly considered it nothing more then Fascism to try and do so. Morality started deep within the soul of each individual. That soul or that person then shared their life with other like-minded individuals that resulted in a neighborhood, then village-next, community, ending in a society with morals or a root-bound stance, which was then called morality. It came from within, on a voluntary basis- not from legislation shoved through by a bunch of politicians eager to jump on any bandwagon as a means to an end...the end always being re-election.

And when the religious right wing started criticizing the President, Bud thought;

"Well, why not? He's there isn't he? Isn't it human nature to criticize the one at the top...king of the mountain and all that stuff? Well, wasn't it?" So Bud spoke out against everything the President did or didn't do.

"He hadn't pulled any punches," he told his constituency, and they agreed and encouraged him to be more outspoken.

"Why not?" he reasoned, it was all for the good of the country. Wasn't it?"

Not really. It was all for the good of Bud Johnson.

He had made, their list, the religious right wing's list. They published that list of candidates for political office, and incumbents they supported. No one really had to look. Everyone knew Bud's name would not only be on it, but highlighted.

Bud not only went along but helped along many of their chosen candidates.

A conspiracy? he wondered, *So what? Who cares? The world is full of conspiracies.*

But when they gathered their elected forces and tried to overturn the national election of the President of the United States, Bud saw clearly, for the first time, up front and personal, how power in the hands of any group can turn good intentioned people into a ruthless, unscrupulous mob.

Power, in the hand of human beings, corrupts. Absolute power in the hands of human beings, absolutely corrupts. And the right wing, those moral watchdogs of the nation had become the most corrupt of all.

Worse they were using their religious name in an all out attempt to crucify a man for doing what many of them had done or were still doing. And Bud Johnson got scared.

Bud hadn't been raised in a deeply religious home. His folks took him to church while he was a kid, and attended occasionally while he was growing up and living in their home. No, he hadn't been raised in a deeply religious home, but his folks taught him to always ask the question, "What would Jesus do?" in any situation, to come up with the correct and right answer...and Bud got scared. Because he didn't think Jesus would be out to crucify another human being.

"Besides", Bud thought, "this is too-too close to what happened in Palestine nearly two thousand years ago." The Pharisees, the right wing conservative, dyed-in-the-wool law enforcers, used their political might to influence the government into crucifying a man...and Bud, got scared.

The President wasn't any Jesus Christ, that was for sure, but he was a human being and Jesus didn't crucify human beings. He prayed for them.

Bud began to wonder about what type of presidency, what type of leadership...what could have been accomplished if the right wing had spent all their energy praying for the president, instead of spending all their energy in an all out attempt to destroy him. What if they had spent all that time praying for him? Bud got scared because he knew, first hand, up-front and personal, that there was definitely an "Anti-Christ...Anti-love...Anti-grace" spirit running rampant in the nation's capital.

Bud always knew, that when the end justified the means, that was demonic...and Bud, got scared.

He withdrew his support of their agenda to get the President at any cost, and spoke out against them. That, he knew, would almost, most assuredly, result in his not being re-elected for another term.

"Well," he thought, "I still have my law degree." He reasoned that he could always, hook up with some law firm and survive, if not thrive, once back in the "real world" again.

But who would be here in this empty house to share his life? What was life, if you didn't have someone to share it with?

The empty house was Bud's doing and Bud's alone. Adultery sounded so acceptable and almost "hip" when you called it an extra-marital affair, and that's what Bud called it for over six months. Not only adultery on his, but on her part as well. Both of them were married and both had children and responsibilities to those kids, let alone their spouses.

But self-gratification can take on a power of its own. It can cloud the truth and kill the spotlight which shines on home and family. Satisfaction is it's reasoning, but it is never satisfied. One night, and then two, three weeks, and then four, three months and then six. Would it still be going on if they had not been caught? Probably...no most assuredly...most assuredly, yes!

Now Ann was gone, with the kids...and life was empty. And what was life, if you didn't have someone to share it with?

Bud stood up from the kitchen table finally, placed his cup of cold coffee in the sink and walked upstairs. Why? He didn't have the slightest idea. That is, not until he saw the rope hanging from the door.

Chapter Eight
ANTICIPATION

Terry headed home for his family's early evening gathering on the verandah and Jerrey rushed home to get cleaned up for the evening. Cleaned up for the evening? That's all he needed, another evening of eating. Half the drive-in-relatives had left already, returning to their own places, leaving a remnant to venture out and stuff themselves again, this time at one of the local Italian restaurants in town. He, of course, had to go along. At least he wouldn't have to worry about another chopped up if not chewed on turkey drumstick leg and dumb purple stuff. Good old spaghetti and meat balls would be what he would order tonight, thank you very much.

Both Terry and Jerrey had looked like beginners on the golf course that afternoon. What with slices by Terry, and Jerrey never able to get across one water trap, it was a day of "Give-mees", and score card lies.

"Jerrey, how was your day?" his mother asked just as the family sat down at one of the restaurant's largest tables. "Great, Mom, and yours?" "Oh," she said, "it was a good day." And off she went. Jerrey knew his mother would take that question and run with it for at least fifteen minutes. His Dad looked across the table at him as if to say, "Way to go son, now we're all going to have to listen to this for God knows how long."

That was fine with Jerrey. It would give him time to think. Yes, think. Jerrey had learned, a long time ago, to think while his mother was talking. She knew he did that, because sometimes she would tell him ridiculous stuff and he would agree only to see her start laughing at him. Like the time he was thinking about something else and she told him his

77

beautiful car had just caught on fire. She asked him if that was okay, and he had said "Yes, of course," only to see her start laughing. But this time she was talking to the left over relatives and not at him. So Jerrey's mind slipped out of the restaurant and back to the day's activities.

The Man. He had seen him again during the day. He was sure of it. Where? - Around Shelley's restaurant. That's where it was. What was he doing around there? How had he disappeared so quickly? Oh, yeah, Alice and Betsy had interrupted their chase. They had lost sight of him because of them. What if he was wrong? What if this guy wasn't who Jerrey thought he was? Why had he allowed Terry to talk him into playing golf? Playing golf? PLAYING GOLF? FOR CHRIST'S SAKE!

"What do you think about that Jerrey"? his mother asked.

Think about what? Jerrey worried. What do I think about playing golf when there's a stalker loose and hair-brain Habersham has me playing golf. Think about what? He had to say something and quick.

"Oh, Mom...well I don't know, I'm not sure." And the entire table bust out laughing. He looked around and everyone at the table was looking at him. He looked over at his Dad who simply gave him a wink as though to say, "Gotcha".

By the time Terry made it home, the others had already gathered on the verandah. He wasn't late, though. You were never late to the family's daily gathering. It was a ritual you made on time.

"Good evening, Mr. Habersham," Mary said, as he stepped onto the verandah.

"Evening, Mary," Terry said with great care and appreciation, taking the drink she handed him.

"Did you have a good day?" he asked her, knowing she appreciated the question.

"It's been a fine day, fine day", Mary answered, thinking how he was following in his grandfather and father's footsteps.

As he turned towards the others on the verandah already sipping their drinks, his father asked,

"Did you and Jerrey catch those girls you were chasing today, son?"

Betsy had a smile on her face you could see through the straw she was sucking on, and Gwen looked like she had just swallowed a chaser cat. Terry thought quickly that it would be easier to go along with their fun then try and explain Jerrey Walker's sightings.

"No sir, didn't. But we're going lookin' again tomorrow."

"That Jerrey sure is turning out to be a looker," Gwen said, raising her eyebrows.

"Cut it out, Gwen," her mother said. "Jerrey's too young for you."

"Nooo he isn't, Mama," Gwen said, flipping her hair flirtatiously. "I stood beside Jerrey today," she continued, "and Jerrey isn't too young for any woman anymore."

They all had to laugh. Gwen had that way about her. She could bring out the laughter in anyone, especially the family, and especially Dad. Lord, she must have taken a bath in that lilac again.

In the midst of their laughter Betsy spoke up and said, "Alice Watts is pregnant."

"Is she? Oh, how wonderful," Evelyn said excitedly.

"About three months," Betsy continued.

"Well, we know what the preachers been doing at nights," Gwen said.

"Hush up, Gwen," Mrs. Habersham said, waving her free hand.

"Well, Grandma, it's okay for preachers to--"

"Gwen," her father interrupted just in time, "how was the "stinkum" business this Friday after Thanksgiving?"

"Great, Daddy!" she said. "We did more business today then...", and off she went.

Dad knew how to get her started. Ask her about business and the flirtatious southern belle was shoved aside by the career businesswoman.

Terry stood on the verandah with the others, sipping their drinks and enjoying the evening's sunset, until his eyes caught Betsy's. Something was wrong. He could see it in her eyes. He had always been able to, and she knew it. She turned away slowly from the others and walked thoughtfully towards the other end of the verandah, knowing he would follow. They met at the opposite end of the verandah, away from the others and looked out over the rippling fields of tall grass. Without warning and without looking at him she said, "Grandma doesn't have long to live, Terry."

It was a shock, but not an overwhelming one. Grandma was really getting up there in years. He knew her years were numbered.

"Well, she's getting up there. One of these days," he said.

"That's not what I mean, Terry," Betsey responded, and Terry realized she was saying something different.

"Well, how long does she have sis?" Terry asked, without looking at his sister.

"Few days at the most," Betsy responded.

"What?" Terry asked, this time turning towards Betsy.

"You heard right, Terry. A few days at the most," Betsy said, as she looked him in the eyes.

"But she seems so healthy and all," Terry said.

"Isn't that wonderful," Betsy responded, turning to look across the verandah at her Grandmother standing with the others.

"Isn't that wonderful." she repeated.

"Does she know?" Terry asked.

"Sure she knows," Betsy replied.

"Do Dad and Mom know?" Terry asked

"Everyone knows Terry. Everyone. You're the last to know,"
Betsy answered.

"Mary?" Terry asked.

"Mary knows," Betsy nodded.

Suddenly Terry felt...empty. He didn't know how to feel. Everyone knew he was the last to know. Grandma even knew. Just a few days? They all seemed so happy standing there talking, and they all knew. Grandma was dying...Grandma.

Mary brought Terry another drink just then and smiling up at him said;

"Here, Terry. It's a beautiful evening, isn't it?"

Terry took the drink from her and turned his back on all of them. He looked out across the fields Grandpa had cleared. He looked down and put his free hand on the white wood railing that ran around the verandah. Wood Grandpa had handled. And tears filled his eyes as he tried to sip his drink. Betsy was on one side and Mary on the other. They stood there for a long time. Silently. Remembering. And the sun went down as they watched...and the sun went down.

Ashley and Sammy had spent most of the afternoon walking all over town, Sammy said. Shelley had assured Katherine it was safe to do so. Yes, Katherine had suspected, and confirmed during one of the day's slow times that, in fact, their waitress and landlord, was the one and only Shelley, owner and main waitress at "Shelley's Restaurant."

Katherine sat in the bathtub soaking, while the kids listened to the furnished radio in the living room. She thought back over the day's activities in wonder. She had planned on, "getting it together MONDAY." And all this had happened without her planning. She hadn't anticipated any of it. What if they had not stepped into the restaurant downstairs early that morning? Wasn't it Ashley who pushed her to do so? What if they had missed all of this? This apartment. This job...this warm water. Too many good things were happening to them. It couldn't be by accident, could it? No. Something was going on. Something was happening. She knew it, but she couldn't figure out what...and Katherine, tired and relaxed, lay back in the warm water and closed her eyes.

As Ashley tucked Sammy into his new bed, his eyes closed. She leaned over and gave him a kiss on the cheek, which he never felt. He was already asleep. She looked down at him and thought, "kid brothers can be okay." She tip toed out of his room, closed the door half way and sat down on the living room couch. She knew that her mother was still soaking in the bathtub. "Good, Let her soak. She deserves it." And Ashley's eyes closed as she lay down on the couch.

The fellowship hall was warm and dry in the woman's shelter and all four of them had eaten a delicious dinner earlier, provided today by Karl Watt's church. As Tom and Jill zipped their two children into the sleeping bags the Church had provided, they knew that tomorrow would be even better. How, they didn't know, they just felt it. Today meant so much to both of them. Tom had planned on returning to the, men's shelter across town, but Karl Watts had worked it out so he could spend the night with his family here.

They kissed their children goodnight and, after a few minutes, slipped over to one of several tables still set up in the fellowship hall. There they joined other shelter guests to share coffee, donuts and, no doubt, part of their stories. When Tom and Jill sat down they both noticed another man sitting at their table. At first Tom thought it strange. This was a woman's shelter. What was he doing here? But then Jill whispered that he was probably the result of Karl Watt's work again. After all, it was Karl who had worked it out so that Tom could spend the night with his family. They both wanted to ask the man at the table, but thought it rude to do so. They drank coffee, ate donuts and talked...and talked...and talked.
At one point Tom looked over at Jill and said, "Remember Karl saying, In the name of Jesus Christ, you are forgiven?" Jill shook her head yes and Tom added, "Wow"...and they both held each other's hand even tighter.
Practically everyone sitting at the table had something to say about the day, even Tom and Jill, but the other man sitting there just smiled, drank coffee, ate donuts, and listened. "The quiet type," thought Jill. Well, there was no obligation to speak. It wasn't a requirement, thought Tom. After a while they all said their good nights and headed back over to the sleeping bags. Right before he zipped himself into the sleeping bag, Tom sat up on one elbow and looked to see

where, "the quiet man", in the dark brown overcoat and bright red scarf wrapped around his neck had gone. Maybe in the morning he could introduce himself, and-but he must have left. Tom didn't see him anymore.

Chapter Nine
RELATIONSHIPS

Saturday

Terry Habersham had graduated from high school at seventeen. During his last year at Etowah High he was also enrolled in Metro Junior College. After junior college came Emory, and Law School. He had his education behind him, his license to practice, and a position in a very small law firm in town by the time he was twenty-three. Terry was a 'brain', and most people in town knew it. They also knew that if he put his mind to it, he could be just about anything or do just about anything he wanted in life.

But all Terry wanted to do was enjoy life. He wasn't out to build any monuments or stuff any banks with his surplus income. He just wanted to play golf, practice law in the small firm, and enjoy life. Of the three, playing golf was his favorite. He wasn't sure if it was the beauty and solitude of the course or the game itself. He just liked playing golf.

His closest friend was Jerrey Walker. Jerrey was four years younger then Terry, but that didn't seem to bother either of them. They had met on the golf course years ago during a junior tournament when Jerrey served as Terry's caddy. What Jerrey didn't know about golf Terry did, and together they made a perfect team. Most caddys are supposed to know a great deal about the game, and especially their course. But that always bothered Terry. He wanted the caddy to keep him company, not give him pointers, and since Jerrey knew very little about the game, let alone the course they were playing, it made for a perfect team and immediate friendship, as far as Terry was concerned. Besides, it was fun running around with Jerrey Walker. The guy was crazy at times, especially over that car of his.

Slowly Terry also taught him the wonderful game of golf. Well, tried to teach him the game. Jerrey was always thinking about something else instead of what he was doing at the time with a golf ball.

Like yesterday chasing after "the invisible man." Lord, what would his dad say if he knew what they had really been doing yesterday? He could hear it even now,

"Son, you're a man of the law now, a young attorney with a great future in this county. You need to watch yourself."

"Bunk!" Terry said out loud as he sat at the kitchen table drinking his morning coffee.

"What was that Mr. Terry?" Mary asked.

"Oh, nothing Mary. Just thinkin'. Has everyone else, already left for the day? And stop that, 'Mr. Terry,' stuff will you, Mary? This is not 'Gone with the wind,' and you ain't, 'Ms Daisy.'

Mary laughed at Terry's comment, and herself, and answered,

"Yes, they're all gone. Your two sisters have gone to work, and your Mama and Daddy have gone shopping downtown. You're the last one in here this morning."

Terry glanced at the clock on the wall. Seven o'clock in the morning and the family had already dispersed for the day.

As his Grandma entered the kitchen Mary went on,

"Betsy had a wonderful idea this morning. She thought it would be a nice gesture to invite Rev. Watts and his wife over for afternoon snakes on the verandah, her being pregnant and all. Then Gwen suggested inviting your friend Jerrey and his parents over. Your Daddy and Mama suggested we ask Bud Johnson to join us, so looks like for the first time I can remember, we're going to have a little party on the verandah this afternoon."

As Mary spoke, she looked at Terry with her eyebrows raised. He knew what she had just said was not only for his ears but for his grandma's as well.

85

"All right!" Terry said. "Now that sounds like a great idea, Mary!"

"Well, don't give me credit. Was the family's idea and a good one at that, I think."

"What about it, Grandma? What do you think?"

"Well, the verandah has always been for Family, but I guess this one time it will be okay. Just once."

Mary winked at Terry as his Grandma spoke.

"Well, great!" Terry said, as he rose from the table.

"See you'll later then," he said as he gave his grandma and Mary a peck on the cheek each, and walked out of the kitchen.

All three of them knew why there was going to be a party tonight on the verandah. All three of them knew.

Alice smiled at herself as she fried the bacon and eggs, smelling up the entire house. Saturday morning breakfast was a family tradition at the Watt's. "Family tradition" she thought, and her smile grew even broader. Then she laughed out load.

Alice had waited 'til they arrived at the arena last evening to tell Karl she was pregnant. In fact she had waited 'til the game was three quarters through.

Well, he had come home so late in the afternoon she had begun to worry about him. He always liked to leave early so they could get to the arena and just 'hang out,' as he called it. As far as she was concerned the hanging out part was a bore, though she had never said anything to the contrary. When he finally did get home to pick her up, it was so late she wondered if they were going or not. But he had rushed in, grabbed his cap, cooler and her, and off they had gone to the game.

She had planned on a nice relaxing afternoon where they would leave in plenty of time to hang out at the game and, somewhere between their house and the arena, she had planned on telling him. But it didn't work out that way, and so she had decided to make him suffer and wait. It took 'til the game was half- way through for her to realize that he wasn't suffering or waiting on anything. He didn't have any idea she had such a surprise for him.

There she was trying to get him upset for upsetting her plans, and he didn't even know it. And on top of that, he didn't even know she had plans in the first place.

"Men"!

Then it had dawned on her that she could really have some fun. So, she waited.

It was during one of the breaks, one of those precious silent moments; standing in the bleachers along with forty three thousand other crazy fans. They had just finished yelling and screaming when she grabbed his hand, leaned over, and said directly into his ear so he would be sure to hear her, "I'm pregnant!"

She'll never forget the look on his face, nor the sound of his half hoarse from yelling during the game, voice.

He looked at her like someone had just told him that he was going to be an astronaut, just as soon as he had his belly button removed. His mouth dropped opened, he actually moved two or three feet away from her and looked down at her waist, and then widened his mouth so large at first, she was sure he was going to dislodge his jaw, and then she was glad no one from the Church was around to see. He yelled loud enough for three rows in front and three in the back to hear;

"YOU'RE PREGNANT...BUT...BUT HOW? I MEAN WHEN? ARE YOU SURE? WHO TOLD YOU? YOU'RE PREGNANT?

By that time at least fifty people had turned to look at them. Most had smiles on their faces and were laughing but not all of them, and on top of it all, some were looking at her with an accusing eye. She knew what they were thinking and so she said;

"YES...I'M THREE MONTHS PREGNANT REVERAND WATTS...AND THE BABY IS YOURS! WHAT ARE YOU GOING TO DO ABOUT IT?"

With that, everyone caught on and began to laugh at Karl who just looked dumbfounded. Then his face turned red as a beet, tears welled up in his eyes and he moved back towards her and gave her one of his famous hugs, amidst the applause of those listening. Finally after gaining his composure, he kissed her right there in front of God and everybody and turned to all of them and bowed. He actually bowed...and they applauded.

She laughed out loud as she placed the bacon plate on the kitchen table and called,

"Daddy Karl,...breakfast."

Karl wore a big smile on his face as he walked into the kitchen and took his seat. They both laughed at one another as they joined hands for the blessing.

"Thank you God for this day of life...and for the life that grows within my wife, who I love so much." Karl was about to say, "Amen", and end his prayer but then he said,

"and God, take care of my wife for pulling such a dirty trick on me last night in front of all those people...Amen." And they both laughed again.

As you can imagine, breakfast that morning was special in the Watt's home. They were both sitting at the kitchen table enjoying each other's company and finishing their second cup of coffee when the phone rang.

"Hello," Alice said.

"Alice, this is Betsy, I'm at the hospital." And a sudden chill came over Alice. Why would Betsy be calling this early on a Saturday morning? The morning after she had...

"Alice, don't worry. Oh, my! I just realized...calling you this early on a Saturday morning...the morning after you just found out...no, no....everything's fine Alice...everything's okay. I just called to invite you and Karl over this evening."

Alice's heart was already pounding in her chest. She reached over and grabbed the back of her chair and pulled it over and sat down slowly. Karl sensed that something was wrong and asked,

"What's wrong Alice?"

Alice caught her breath and replied,

"Nothing...nothing. It's Betsy."

As she spoke, her voice relaxed and Karl read the situation and knew what had just happened. Alice went on,

"They want us to come over this evening around five thirty or six?" It was both a question, to confirm the time with Betsy and information for Karl.

"Sure, we'd love to Betsy", he said loud enough for Betsy to hear across the table and over the phone.

"I've been trying to get that family to church for months."

Alice said, "Karl"...

Betsy said, "I heard that. Well, here's your chance."

As Karl stood to leave the kitchen, knowing the two women would be on the phone for awhile, he leaned over to his wife, and she cupped her hand over the telephone's mouth piece as he said,

"When Betsy called just then and you were frightened, God got you back for last night. Gotcha'...gotcha'...gotcha'! God works in mysterious ways...gotcha'."

Alice kept her hand over the phone to keep Betsy from hearing her laugh as Karl left the kitchen saying over and over: "Gotcha'...gotcha'...gotcha'."

Jerrey had been up since six a.m. A seven-thirty appointment at his favorite local garage to have his "beautiful car" worked on was the reason. Oil change and all four tires rotated.

While he was showering the questions started coming again. In fact they had bombarded him through out the night. Who was the man he had seen on Thursday standing in line? At first he thought he knew, now he wasn't sure. Why had he seen him on Friday, close to Shelley's restaurant? How had he disappeared so quickly? Was he looking for the man, or was he just interested in the girl? She was cute, but so what? Maybe if he found her, he'd find the man. Was the man stocking the small family? Why? Why in the world was this stuff bothering him so? Why not just forget it and go on to something else? Why couldn't he get it out of his head? On and on it went, over and over. On the way down to the garage the entire cycle started again. It was driving him crazy.

When he pulled up to the garage at seven fifteen for his seven thirty appointment, thank you very much, George, the lead mechanic and owner, said they would be running about an hour behind. Overnight drop-offs and such. Jerrey didn't say anything to George about running behind, he had known George for years. Honest as the day is long, that was George. And besides, it was George who had helped restore and beautify his "beautiful car." Jerrey said not to worry, and that he'd be back in a little bit to pick up his "beautiful car." You could smell "Shelley's" cinnamon rolls all the way up to "George's Auto." And so, as planned the night before with Terry, Jerrey headed in that direction.

It was quite this early in the morning downtown. But that would soon change. If Friday the day after Thanksgiving was the biggest shopping day of the year, Saturday had to come in a close second. That's why he had planned on having his car worked on and out of downtown before the stores opened and the rush started.

As he walked the broad sidewalk along Main Street, led by the sweet aroma of cinnamon rolls, he glanced once again at his downtown. Jerrey had lived here all his life. In fact he had been born at the local hospital, just three blocks away from where he was walking. Born at seven-thirty in the morning. What time was it now? Seven-thirty. Well what-da-ya-know? The rest of his family couldn't say that. Why? Because they had all been born elsewhere. In fact, they had all been raised elsewhere.

Jerrey's folks had moved here a year or two before he was born, he couldn't remember which. No, this was his town, so to speak, and he loved it. While Main Street in his town may be considered by some to be a typical Southern main street, Jerrey thought different.

"How many Main streets," he thought as he walked along, "are lined with such beautiful old buildings and kept up like these are? Why, they look new but they aren't. They were all here before I was born. What a great place, this town of mine."

Jerrey glanced into the storefront windows as he walked along the quiet streets. Some of the owners were turning on lights, straightening up and preparing for the day's rush as he walked by. Most of them knew him and waved as he walked by. They guessed where he was headed: everyone loved Shelley's cinnamon rolls.

As he grew closer to "Shelley's", the sweet aroma and anticipation increased to the point that he ignored the traffic light and started to cross the street without looking. A blast of siren from the patrol car startled him and he froze in place. Everyone in "Shelley's" heard the siren and looked out through the huge windows.

"Better not J-walk this early in the morning, Jerrey," the patrolman said from the driver's seat of his patrol car, a smirk on his face.

Just then the light changed and the sign indicated "walk", so Jerrey Walker, with everyone inside "Shelley's" looking at him, crossed the street in front of the patrol car and walked into the restaurant.

"Good of you to let us know you were comin' Jerrey," Shelley said, and the restaurant erupted with laughter.

Embarrassed somewhat, but used to the harassment, he looked for Terry and saw him sitting at a table near the front.

"You always arrive with such fanfare?"

"Shut up," Jerrey said as he pulled out one of the chairs and sat down.

"Coffee?" Shelley mouthed to Jerrey from across the restaurant. "Yes," he mouthed back, and he knew they would be on their way.

"Morning, siren man," Shelley said as she sat down his steaming hot cup of coffee and slid a plate with two huge cinnamon rolls in front of him.

"What brings you downtown so early in the morning? Not that I'm not glad to see you. Been a while, Jerrey."

"Gettin my car worked on," he answered.

"You mean that, "beautiful car" needs workin' on?"

"Yep. That's why it's so beautiful. I keep it looking that way."

"That you do young man, that you do," Shelley said as she walked over to another table and re-filled their coffee cups.

"You gonna' eat both of those?" Terry asked

"Want one?" Jerrey asked.

"Nope. Couldn't get out of the house this morning without eating some of Mary's biscuits. I'm stuffed." Terry answered.

"I've been thinking," Jerrey said.

"Lord help us," Terry responded.

"This guy we're looking for. I know I've seen him before somewhere. Or, at least I think I've seen him before somewhere."

"Well, that took a lot of thought,." Terry said. "How long did you say you'd been thinking about this?"

"Shut up and listen, smart-alek. Maybe I haven't seen him before," Jerrey went on, "but I think I have."

"Well, that clarifies everything," Terry responded.

"What if he has one of those faces that fits in, but stands out?" Jerrey went on

"Have you been drinking?" Terry asked.

"I'm serious, Terry!" Jerrey said in desperation.

Terry leaned over the table and said softly, "Listen pal, I know you're serious. But you're letting this thing get the best of you. Now, cool down. Eat your fat-free breakfast and we'll look...after while."

"I heard that 'fat-free' stuff," Shelley said as she walked up to the table and refilled both their cup

"Shelley's" restaurant was open from six a.m. till seven p.m., six days a week, closed on Sunday's. While the restaurant didn't open 'til six a.m., preparations started at four-thirty. The same was true for closing, though it didn't take as long

92

to close. Katherine and Shelley had left the restaurant at about seven-thirty the night before. Shelley headed for her home in the suburbs while Katherine climbed the steps to her new apartment, dead tired. It had been a long day.

Suddenly she sat straight up in bed wondering where she was. Then she remembered. It was her new bed, in her new apartment. "The kids" she thought. She rolled out of bed, wrapped a blanket around herself and opened the door to her bedroom that she didn't remember closing, and stepped into the living room.

"Hi mom." Ashley said with a big smile on her face. "Have a good sleep?"

"Y-e-s" Katherine said as she looked around the living room for Sammy. Reading her mother's mind, Ashley said,

"He's playing with his boat in the bathtub."

"Oh, good," Katherine responded as she walked over and curled up on the couch.

"Shelley said she could use some help around ten. I offered to help but she said maybe later, after I got settled in school and all."

"What time is it?" her Mother asked.

"Eight-fifteen." Ashley answered.

"You spoke to Shelley this morning?" Katherine asked.

"Yep. I smelled the cinnamon rolls baking and went down. Sammy was sound asleep like you, and there's only one way in and out of this apartment, and that's through the restaurant. Shelley gave me one of her cinnamon rolls, and I brought one up for you and Sammy. He's already eaten his. Yours is in the kitchen. Want it?"

"Yes." Katherine answered as she moved from the couch toward the kitchen. There in the middle of the kitchen table was a dinner plate, with the largest cinnamon roll on it Katherine had ever seen. It covered the entire plate. Ashley read her mother's mind and said,

"Big enough Mom? And you wait Mom, they are delicious. No wonder people come here for Shelley's cinnamon rolls. Sammy couldn't eat all of his so I wrapped it up for him. It's over there on the stove," Ashley said as she nodded towards the plate.

"Try it," she said as her mother sat down at the table. Ashley had placed a folk beside the monster cinnamon roll earlier, after bringing it up from downstairs. As her mother took her first bite, Ashley poured her a glass of milk from the carton Shelley had given her earlier. It was nice sitting there at the kitchen table watching her mother devour the cinnamon roll. It was nice waking up in their own place.

The hospital had phoned Betsy before she left the Ranch and asked if she would drop by the Mary Weather senior citizen complex on her way in. Of course she had agreed to do so. All the doctors at the hospital took their turn at Mary Weather. It was the only senior citizen complex in town and theirs was the only county hospital. After examining the guest at Mary Weather, she prescribed some mild medication and drove on to the hospital arriving at approximately eight-thirty.

After assuring herself that her two colleagues in the emergency room had everything under control, she pulled her grandmothers file again for, one more look. She had reviewed the file several times by now, "but one never knew," she told herself. No new revelations. No oversights. No rediscoveries. It looked the same as yesterday, and the day before, and the day before that. Grandma didn't have long. Not long at all.

When Betsy first discovered the problem she had planned on radical treatment for Grandma. But in the midst of laying out her plans she stopped, knowing her grandmother would never go along with them. She would have said something like: "Too much effort and fuss...and for what?" And maybe Grandma was right. In any event, no medication would work now. Not now. Now, it was too late-too late.

Nurse Kim brought Betsy back to reality with a touch to her shoulder.

"Tom and Jill Smith are here." Nurse Kim said, reminding Betsy of their scheduled visit.

"Where are they?" she asked.

"In room six," Nurse Kim answered.

As Betsy walked slowly toward the examining room, her thoughts shifted from her grand mother to this couple waiting on her. Was medicine all she had to offer this couple? It wasn't her job to pry or meddle. It wasn't her job to be a spiritual guide or counselor, though patients often asked her advice. Her job was to be a medical doctor, to examine, evaluate, and prescribe treatment. But Tom and Jill seemed different. They had both made a serious mistake. Oh yes, she knew their story. But in their case, bitterness had not set in. Nor were they angry at each other. In fact, their love was still strong for one another. If only she could help, but she didn't know how nor what to do except be their doctor.

When Betsy entered the room Tom was sitting in the chair and Jill was sitting on the examining table. Both were talking a mile a minute.

"Good morning," Betsy said.

"Morning," t

They both responded.

"And how are things?" Betsy inquired, the next question in her usual sequence.

"Great!" they both said.

"You won't believe what has happened," Tom said.

Betsy didn't think she could have stop Tom from telling her even if she wanted to and, as he went on, she didn't want to.

When he got to the part about Rev. Karl Watts, Betsy couldn't help but smile.

"God, you are something else," she thought as Tom and Jill both now told Betsy all that had happened to them since Thanksgiving day.

"God, you are something else."

Though he would never admit it, especially out loud to his closest friend, rrey admired Terry Habersham. Not only was Terry older and smarter, he had graduated early and was practicing law already. Jerrey hadn't even started college yet. Didn't know if he wanted to and, if so, what he would study. It wasn't that he didn't want to go to college. He just didn't know what for. Terry always seemed to be focused, while Jerrey wondered around aimlessly, or at least he thought so. Secretly though, he admired Terry. If only he could be that focused, or that smart. He had never said anything to his friend and never would.

"I mean, how does a guy my age, say to another guy, 'I admire you.'" Jerrey asked himself, and since he didn't know the answer to his own question he kept quiet and didn't say anything.

Now here they sat in, "Shelley's" early on a Saturday morning, two close friends: the mentor lawyer and the wondering hopeful, planning to search for a man they didn't know, and for what neither had the slightest idea. Jerrey was after the man because...he really didn't know why, he just had to find him, and Terry was becoming interested in the hunt because of the challenge.

"This guy you're...we're after," Terry corrected himself, "he's like the Loch Ness monster."

"Yeah, and I'll bet he can play golf, too," Jerrey responded.

"Would you look at that?" Terry said as he looked out the storefront glass window from "Shelley's". There, walking down the sidewalk was a bundle of boxes. It looked like a box collage. He had never seen any one person carrying that many boxes in his life.

"Now who in the world...?" Terry started to say, but stopped in mid sentence when he realized the collage, was being carried by his own mother. As she walked by the front of "Shelley's," she dropped a box. This unfortunate accident accumulated when she tried to pick up the fallen box while trying to maintain control of all the others. This act resulted in the second box falling, soon to be followed by the third, fourth and so on. In front of everyone in the restaurant, everyone outside who cared to look, his mother dropped every single box she had been carrying right there on the sidewalk, and then just stood there for a minute or two, looking at them, as though to say, "Well, pick yourselves up now." Terry, embarrassed at and for his mother jumped up from his chair, and was headed out the front door, when he saw his father cross the street, and run to his mother's aid. Terry and his father arrived at the scene of the accident, and picked up the boxes, sharing the load between the two of them. With both hands full, Terry's father said, "Evelyn, I told you to wait and I'd be right back." "Well, I thought I could handle them Ted," she replied. Realizing for the first time that Terry was there with them she said, "Terry, where did you come from?"

"Shelley's", he answered.

At that, all three of them looked in through the big store front window at Jerry Walker sitting there with half a cinnamon roll on his plate and what appeared to be the other half stuffed in his mouth, washing it down with a cup of coffee.

"Hi, Jerrey." Evelyn said as she waved from the sidewalk. And though he couldn't hear her, Jerrey, a little embarrassed and feeling on stage, waved back.

"Come on, let's go in and have a cup of coffee or something." Terry said as he walked with half of his mother's load in through the front door of the restaurant. Not having any choice in the matter, his mother and father followed him in to the restaurant and over to where Jerrey was sitting.

"Got quite a load there," Jerrey said with a smirk on his face.

"Doing a little Christmas shopping early, Jerrey," Evelyn said, as she unbuttoned her coat and sat down.

"Well, was it good?" she asked, pointing to the cinnamon roll remains.

"Yes ma'am it was," Jerrey answered.

"Want one?" Shelley asked as she stood there with her pen at the ready.

"Oh, no thanks Shelley. Just coffee for me." she answered.

"And me too, please," Terry's father added.

"Well, you guys are up and at it early for a Saturday morning," Terry's father said.

"We just couldn't help ourselves father. We had to get here early so we could watch all the shoppers," Terry responded.

"Jerrey, you try real hard now not to follow in your friend's smart-alek foot steps," Ted said.

"I'll try Mr. Habersham, but it's not easy," Jerrey answered, amused at Terry's father.

"Hey, Jerrey. There's your folks!" Ted said. "Let's invite them to join us," he added as the jumped up from his chair and proceeded to wave Jerrey's folks into the restaurant.

After greeting one another, skirmishing around for loose furniture, pilling boxes upon boxes and unbuttoning coats, the participants of this impromptu gathering added chairs and another table, then finally took their seats.

"Well, good to see you all again, Ted, Evelyn," Jerrey's Dad said.

"Yes, same here Burt. How was Thanksgiving, Nancy?" Terry's father asked.

And so the small talk continued between their folks. Jerrey looked across the table at Terry and they both smiled. It wasn't as though neither could believe it. This sort of thing happened all the time in Jerrey's town. "Small towns are like that," he thought. People see friends and drop everything sometimes just to share a cup of coffee or drink a cool drink and talk. So there they sat, listening to the four old friends reminisce.

"Did Gwen phone you?" Terry's father asked.

"No, but we just left her store. She was saying something about getting together this evening over at your place?" Jerrey's Dad said in a questioning manner.

"Yes, and....."

Terry's father elaborated on this evening's plans as Terry and Jerrey nodded to one another and stood simultaneously.

"Where y'all going?" Jerrey' mother asked.

"Got to go, mom. Important things to do," Jerry answered.

"Good to see y'all...see you this evening," Terry added as both headed for the front door. Just as Terry turned back to close the door behind him Shelley, standing near the back of the restaurant, held up the two boys' ticket. Terry motioned toward the gathering he had just left and mouthed, "Give it to my father." Shelley nodded and smiled knowing Terry had just pulled one on the old man again. How many times, over the years, had he stuck his Dad with the bill? She couldn't remember. Whatever the count was, she had just been told to add one more. She couldn't wait for the fun.

As the two men talked about little or nothing, as far as the women were concerned, Evelyn leaned over the table and said,

"Jerrey's growing up to be a fine young man, Nancy."

"Thank you Evelyn, but I wish he had his act together like Terry does," Nancy replied.

"Well, he will. Give him time," Nancy replied. It was true wasn't it? she thought. Terry did have his act together didn't he"? She wondered for a moment what those two were up to meeting here this early on a Saturday morning, especially the Saturday right after Thanksgiving. Normally, Terry would be on the golf course by now. Well maybe that was where they were going now. Probably so. "Oh well," she thought, "boys will be boys," and sat there, proud as a peacock.

After Jerrey parked his "beautiful" car in Terry's assigned parking space, the two young men walked up to the front door of Terry's law firm. Well, it wasn't Terry's firm yet. He was just one of the lawyers; but knowing Terry, it would be his eventually if he wanted it.

"I won't be long Jerrey, just have to check on a couple of things," Terry said apologetically.

"No problem," Jerry replied.

As the two young men entered the law offices of "Kimbel and Rice", Terry headed straight to his office as Jerrey lingered behind. Jerrey walked slowly, looking around, smelling the leather and thinking about becoming a lawyer himself. The same thoughts raced thought his mind every time he came to Terry's office. "I could be a lawyer if I wanted," he thought. "Why not? "I've got the brains. Maybe not the brains of Terry Habersham, but I've got brains. I could be a good lawyer. Maybe even take on a case and beat Terry in the courtroom sometime in the future. Why not?" His fantasy continued as he strolled down the plush carpeted hallway to Terry's office.

"What time is it now Ashley?" Katherine asked.

"Nine forty-five, Mom," she replied.

Well, I'd better get downstairs. I'll check on you'll later. Watch Sammy. You be good for Ashley, Sammy," she said as she descended the staircase. Katherine knew she didn't have to give either of them instructions. They both had aged so much over the past few months. More then they should've had to. Maybe now, somehow, she could make it up to them. Let them both be kids again.

At the bottom of the staircase there was a full-length mirror. No doubt put there by Shelley when she lived upstairs. Katherine took a good look at herself in the mirror. She looked acceptable in the uniform Shelley had provided, but the dark rings under her eyes were a dead give-a-way. They shouted, "This woman's been through too much". But Katherine couldn't do anything about the shadows right now. She was so eternally thankful for all that had taken place over the last twenty-four hours. "Just think," she said to herself, "Just yesterday morning we were homeless...and look at us now." She knew if she continued to stand there looking at her self in the mirror, and thinking, she would begin to cry. So she stopped, straightened her dress one last time and walked through the curtains at the back of the restaurant.

The restaurant was about half full. Katherine stood there for a minute taking in the sights, until she spotted Shelley behind the counter. As she walked toward the owner of the restaurant and her landlord, a patron or two lifted their half empty cups of coffee indicating a refill would be appreciated. Katherine nodded and headed for the coffee pot in order to fill their requests.

"Morning," Shelley said with broad smile on her face.

"Morning," Katherine answered.

Two couples were leaving near the front of the restaurant so Katherine headed that way to re-set the tables they had, for some reason, dragged together. People did that a lot yesterday, Katherine reminded herself.

As she refilled coffee cups and re-set tables, Katherine noticed that, slowly, the restaurant emptied. The breakfast crowd was moving on, giving Shelley a needed rest before the lunch crowd arrived.

"I could have come down this morning and helped, Shelley," Katherine said.

"You needed your rest, honey," Shelley said.

"Besides, your be earning your money this afternoon. Saturdays are always busy and on top of it, today is shopping day in this big city. Speaking of money, here's yesterday's pay and a week's advance. Thought you could use it. And there's a little extra in there. Not much, mind you, but enough for the kids to get out and go to a movie this afternoon on me. You can pay the advance back with your tips. Sometimes the tips here are pretty good, sometimes not. Anyway, hand me that pot will you?"

As Katherine took the envelope, She reached for the pot and handed it to Shelley. Katherine wanted to say something but she didn't know what. Thanks would be totally inadequate. How had she come to meet such a gracious person as Shelley? She didn't know. Who was she to thank for the introduction? Katherine opened her mouth to speak and Shelley read her mind.

"It all comes around you know. I came to this town years ago. Didn't know a soul. Some one here gave me a break, honey. I've been waiting for a long time to repay that debt, if there is a debt somewhere. In any case, I've been waiting to help someone out, like I was helped. Then you and the kids walked in yesterday and I knew, some how I just knew, like some one told me, you were the ones. I'm blessed, Katherine. Now it's your turn. Know how to light a steam table?"

"I think so. I'll figure it out. Shelley...Thanks!"

The door opened and in walked six people. Shelley turned to Katherine and said, "Here we go, honey."

Chapter Ten
DISCOVERY

She was dressed, 'To the tee' as they said around here. Conservative, but 'To the tee'. Her black, patent leather high heels forced her to walk almost on her toes, accentuating the calves of her legs, and the black stockings she wore emphasized their length. The black suit she had chosen this morning highlighted her figure, especially since the skirt to the suit was on the short side, and the single strand of white pearls around her neck, given to her by her mother, seemed to rest lightly and invitingly there. Her hazel eyes, which seemed to sparkle with life and question every man's intentions, were captivating, and her shoulder-length hair framed her beautiful face with softness and wonder. She was a portrait in motion, a true Southern beauty. Time and again, men would turn to look at her as she passed by, those who knew her often went out of their way to speak to her, and those who didn't wished they had the courage and a reason to introduce themselves.

She walked out of the front door of her perfumery with confidence. Penny Lou Cook, the full-time employee she had working for her was reliable and 'honest as the day is long', she thought. The two part-time college students she had just hired would do for the holidays, and, besides she could well afford them. Gwen's perfume business had been a hit since she opened the doors four years earlier. Everyone in town knew Gwen liked perfume. She made sure of that by over-spraying her self with Lilac every morning before leaving her bedroom. She liked Lilac and knew everyone had something to say about the amount she wore but, as far as Gwen was concerned, that was 'just good business.' A walking advertisement: "Here I come, Lilac and all...and by the way, did you know I own a perfumery downtown?"

Though Gwen Habersham was a successful businesswoman in the truest sense of the word, and should have been content with her success, she wasn't. Gwen wanted a family. She knew they always said 'You can't have everything in life'. Whoever "they" were, she didn't know, but she had heard that all her life. Well, why not? And who said she couldn't have a family anyway? She had wanted the business and worked hard to make it a success, but she had never said, even to herself, that the business would be a substitute for having a family. She knew Betsy wanted a family also, but was willing to trade that idea in if her career demanded it. Not Gwen. She had worked hard to build her business, but would walk away from it in a heart beat, for the sake of a family...In a heart beat! She wasn't getting any younger, either. She was approaching her mid-twenties and though that was not old, or anything, she wanted to find a man, the right man. She had dated plenty of men. After all, she knew-she had looked in the mirror more then once-she knew she was very attractive. Over the years, she had dated some of the best looking men in the county. But she hadn't found the right one yet. Well, not until this one. This one she thought was the one. She was sure of it. Well, almost sure of it. He was a handsome and successful man who appreciated the finer things of life, including her companionship. They had dated for over a year now and as far as she was concerned, it was getting serious. She thought he felt the same. She hoped he felt the same.

They had planned on having lunch at "Farrison's". A fine, white linen cloth restaurant about two blocks from Gwen's business. As she walked along the Main Street sidewalk, speaking to this person and that one, mostly men who spoke to her first, enjoying the noonday sun, she couldn't help but think about her future. Where did it lie? What was in store for her?

Suddenly, out of the blue, for no reason at all, Jerrey Walker popped into her head and she started to smile. She even laughed a little out loud, no doubt brightening her face even more, so the men folk took even more notice of her as she walked along. She had known Jerry Walker for years. Terry had introduced Jerrey to Gwen right after the two of them had met on the golf course. He was five years younger then Gwen but cute as a button, far as she was concerned, and not bad looking at that. Right from the get-go, she had flirted with Jerrey. She didn't know why, she just had. And it had embarrassed him, which made her want to do it even more. Why, just yesterday when Terry and Jerrey had dropped into her business, she had flirted with him. She laughed again, this time to herself, as she approached "Farrison's." "Jerrey Walker," she said out loud, "What a card."

Jeff was waiting for her just inside the restaurant. He greeted her with a peck on the cheek.

"'Noon, pretty," he said.

"Hi, handsome," Gwen answered, blushing slightly at his remark.

The hostess led them to a small table for two, near the back of the restaurant, close to a window overlooking a little enclosed garden patio.

It was one, if not the most impromptu and in-depth discussions they had both experienced in over a year of dating. After the usual personal reviews and updates, their conversation had shifted to the remaining upcoming Holidays and plans, his plans and hers. The Holiday plans discussion led to other plans. Plans for next year. Plans for her business and his career. The 'Five-year Plan', he was such a slave to, plans for the future, short term and long, and ultimately family plans.

Half way though lunch, in the middle of their conversation; Gwen's eyes began to tear. At first she didn't know why, and blamed it on her allergies. But when it continued and even worsened, she excused herself and went to the lady's room.

After drying her eyes and making sure everything looked proper in the ladies room mirror, she reluctantly admitted to herself the truth. Truth is always there, you know. It journeys with you and lingers in the wings waiting for rediscovery. Truth can be comforting, soothing, and even reassuring. But at times, truth can be so cruel. Gwen had to admit the truth. She had to. She knew why her eyes had started to water. She knew why. The truth had eased in slowly, but most assuredly, during their lunch. Gwen Habersham realized, after a year of dating and planning with Jeff, she realized, she knew, he was not the one...and her eyes filled again...and again...and again.

Maybe she was asking for too much. Maybe she wanted too much. This guy was perfect for her. They were so good together. But the longer she stood there looking in the mirror arguing with herself, the more she realized it was true, and she knew it. Jeff was not the one. "Oh God, why?" she asked, not realizing she already had the answer to her question.

"Three blocks up and over two, 'The Eastland Theater," Shelley had said. Ashley hadn't been to a movie for so long she couldn't remember,' She had said when her mother gave her the news. The fact that she had to take her little brother Sammy along with her didn't matter. Sit upstairs in the apartment watching him, or take him to a movie and watch him there. The movie was the better of the two choices. So she had jumped at the chance. And there it was. "Not a super big movie house, but big enough," she thought as they approached the theater. The movie showing was more for younger kids "But what the heck," she thought as she paid for the tickets. Inside was pretty nice for a small movie house. In the concession area she bought Sammy a bag of popcorn and a small Coke and they entered the theater and settled down for a relaxing Saturday afternoon.

Time catches up with you, eventually. You can stretch it out and even try to outrun it, but eventually it will catch up with you, and snap you back. Sleep is part of time. Sleep restores and refreshes the body, in time. It renews and reenergizes. Like charging a battery, the body must have sleep. Go without sleep for too long, and the body's energy is zapped...the battery goes dead. Fatigue is even more serious. Fatigue is the loss of energy over a long period of time. Stretched to the limit-snap-and the body takes it's rest, in spite of us.

Both Ashley and her mother had struggled through her father's disappearance. Her mother seemed to understand why her father had abandoned them, something about his pride or ego. But Ashley didn't understand. She thought that when a man had kids, he was as responsible for those kids as their mother was. Ego smeego. Who cared about pride, and all that stuff? There was no excuse for her Dad leaving. None! Over the last several weeks their lives had been miserable, all on account of him. He had disappointed her so. Where was her Dad? That bum!

As the teenager and her younger brother settled down in the movie theater's comfortable seats, away from everything, Ashley (Smith) Broden's body snapped, and rushed her into a deep sleep. Pictures of rolling meadows filed with flowers and a little girl saying, "I'm coming Daddy," as she ran through the waist high roses and daffodils, swept into her mind. Sweet music of security filled every space and the quiet flow of waterfalls sent peace through- out her entire being. There was no pain in this place. No hurt. No abandonment. No disappointment. Only joy was allowed here. Happiness watered the flowers and laughter created sweet breezes of bliss. In this place of tranquillity, fear was unknown, for here one experienced true sanctuary: that place where the lion lies down with the lamb. Where friend and foe are of one mind. Where enemies are no more. Where swords are turned into plowshare and guns are melted to frame homes for all. When the little girl running through the flowers reached her Daddy, he swept her up in his arms and hugged her tightly. It had been all too long since her Daddy had embraced the little girl. Safe and secure from all life's harms, surrounded by immeasurable, unconditional love, she could have stayed in his arms forever and ever, but...

"Miss...Miss..." Through the fog of a thousand clouds she began to hear someone, and feel her body being shaken.

"Miss, Miss...it's time to go. Miss..."

Ashley couldn't figure it out at first. Who was it? What were they doing? What did they want?

"Miss...Miss...it's time to go. Miss..."

At first she opened her eyes to see blurs and bumps and then slowly focus came. Where was she? What did they...he want?

Miss...Miss..the movies' over. It's time to go."

"Movie...what Movie?"

"Movie?" Ashley said as she forced herself to sit upright in the theater's seat.

"Sammy!" she said as she looked at the seat next to her and realized he wasn't there.

"Oh, don't worry," the teenager, said. "He's out in the lobby piggen out on popcorn and Coke."

"Who..." Ashley said, still in a daze.

"Come on and stand up, that'll help get you awake," the teenager said as he reached out his hand to her.

He pulled and she struggled, still half a sleep, until she was on her feet.

"Nice sleep, huh?" the teenager said.

"A-yeah, I guess," Ashley managed to say.

They walked slowly out of the empty theater into the concession area where Sammy was having a ball. He was sitting on a stool, behind the counter, eating popcorn out of a cardboard bucket and spilling much of it on the floor around him.

"Sammy, you okay?" was all Ashley could manage to say when she saw him.

"He's fine," the man sweeping up, said.

"He's been having fun. Likes his pop corn and Coke, that's for sure."

"Au...thanks. What do we owe...?"

"You don't owe me anything Miss. He's been fun to be with. Besides, you couldn't afford to pay for all the popcorn he's eaten and Coke he's drank," the man said, unaware of their current financial position.

"Thanks," was all Ashley could say as she helped Sammy down from the stool.

"Might wanna' clean him up a little before you take him home. You can take him in the ladies rest room if you want. There's no one here but us," the man said.

Ashley cleaned and straightened up both of them before leaving the theater. As they walked out into the brightness of the afternoon sun, their eyes struggled to adjust.

Jerrey Walker almost wrecked his, "beautiful car," when he saw them.   There she was, the girl--the daughter of that woman. There she was with her younger brother, the one he had seen standing in line. The one he had made a fool of himself in front of. The one that man was stalking.

"There she is!" he yelled at Terry sitting in the seat next to him. Jerrey made a U-turn in the middle of the street and headed back toward the girl and her brother.

The movie theater sat on a quiet side street, but Ashley could see the cross street up ahead was crowded with shoppers. As she and Sammy walked along the sidewalk, Ashley heard the tires on a car squeal as it made a "U-turn." She looked back toward the noise and saw the car headed right for them. Frightened at the sight in this new strange town, she picked Sammy up in her arms and ran down the sidewalk toward the traffic light and the safety of the crowds. The car followed them and some one was yelling, "Hey! Hey, remember me? Hey, remember?"

Near the corner, and safety, she stopped, put Sammy down on the sidewalk, and snuck a peek at the car's driver as he pulled the car up to the curb right in front of them.

It was that jerk. That jerk who had sat down in front of them at the big church on Thanksgiving day. The jerk that had said he'd seen her dad standing in line with them. The jerk.

"YOU JERK! YOU PERVERT! GET AWAY FROM ME! Ashley yelled.

"No, no, you don't understand," Jerrey tried to explain.

"I DO UNDERSTAND! GET AWAY FROM ME! She yelled again as she drew Sammy closer.

"Listen! I've been worried about you," Jerrey said, as he opened his car door to get out.

Ashley didn't wait. She picked Sammy back up in her arms and ran the short distance to the traffic light and the safety of the crowd standing there. When the light turned and the crowd started to cross the street, she joined them, Sammy in arms. As they arrived on the other side and stepped up onto the curb, the jerk stalking them drove down the street and made another U-turn putting him on the same side of the street as she and Sammy again.

What was she to do? Right here! Right here in front of all these people, this guy was after her! When the light turned again, she picked Sammy back up and crossed, in the safety of the crowd she hoped, to the other side of the street. The jerk-stalker-guy-rapist-assailant, and God knew what else, turned his old polished car at the light and headed down the same street, but on the other side from where they were walking. She felt somewhat safer since there were cars and a lot of people between them.

"HEY!" the rapist yelled again from across the street.

"HEY!", And the sound of metal smashing against metal, glass breaking, and a whimpering, "NO!" filled the early afternoon shopper's ears. Ashley turned to see that the jerk chasing her had smashed his old car into a stopped car in front of him.

"Good for you," she yelled. "You jerk," she added. And she hurried down the sidewalk and around the corner with Sammy, leaving the stalker to cry over his car.

"Jerrey?" The policeman asked. "Are you okay?"

"I'm fine," he answered.

"Terry, you okay?" The policeman asked next.

"I'm fine Tony, "What about...is that Harry Lee and his wife?" Terry asked.

"Sure is," Tony answered. "I've already checked. They're all right."

"Jerrey, what happened?"

"Well Officer Tony, it's like this," Terry butted in.

"My client here was driving along peacefully, being very careful with his, "beautiful car" as usual, when all of a sudden, the brakes gave way, or perhaps his foot inadvertently missed the brake pedal...an unavoidable accident...a no-fault finding. Let the insurance companies work it out"

"UH Huh." Officer Tony said with an unmistakable awareness in his voice.

"And it didn't have a thing to do with that young girl he was following?" The policeman asked.

"Oh, no. Well, I'm not sure about that. You know these young men and their libidos," Terry went on.

"These young men," Tony echoed with a smirk growing on his face as he turned to Jerrey.

"Jerrey, give me your license and insurance card," the policeman said.

"Looks like your attorney here is right. Looks like a no-fault accident to me, too. We'll let the insurance companies fight it out."

Taking the requested cards, Tony turned back to Terry and said, "Better go and check on Harry Lee and his wife, Terry."

It took another half-hour to exchange insurance information, though it was really a waste of time, both were insured by one of Jim Thomason's companies. In fact Jim Thomason had almost everyone in town insured in one of his companies.

Jerrey's "beautiful car," along with Harry Lee's, suffered minor damage. George's garage would have them both, good as new in no time.

After Harry Lee and his wife drove on, Jerrey pulled his once "beautiful car" over to the curb and parked it. He wanted to assess the damage once again. Terry and Tony stood on the sidewalk watching. Finally, after a few minutes, Tony asked,

"What was he doing chasing that girl, Terry? I mean she's new in town. I think he scared her half to death."

110

"Jerrey's been seeing things recently. A man, in fact. One minute he's there and the next, he's gone. Jerrey says he first saw this guy standing next to her, that girl and her mother and brother yesterday. They were standing in line over at the big church." Terry explained.

"He went down and talked with the family Thanksgiving afternoon while they were eating lunch, and they said that they were alone and there wasn't any man with them," Terry went on.

"Isn't that place for women only?" the officer asked.

"Yep. But he swears he saw this guy standing behind them.

"Then yesterday he thought he saw him again down by Shelley's," Terry explained.

"You mean we might have a street person, stalker or something following that family?" Tony asked, putting on his best detective face.

"Could be Tony. Could be."

"Well, I'll keep an eye out for this guy," Tony said. "What's he looking like, exactly?"

"Jerrey, Tony wants a complete description of this guy we've...you've been chasing," Terry yelled to the other side of he car where Jerrey was bemoaning the temporary loss of his car's beauty.

But when he heard Terry, Jerrey stopped whining about his car and walked over to where Terry was standing with Tony. Pleased, to say the least, that someone was finally taking him serious Jerrey, over the next ten minutes, gave officer Tony a very good description of the man following, stalking, the small family. Officer Tony promised to follow up on the matter.

Finally, we might find this guy, Jerrey thought as Tony walked away with his note pad full. He and Terry hopped back into his not-so- "beautiful car", and drove slowly down the street towards the corner where the girl had last appeared.

Karl was waiting for Tom and Jill Smith at the rapid transit station. When they arrived, Karl threw their meager belongings in the back of his jeep, placed the kids in seat belts in the back seat, and hopped in the front with Tom and Jill. The ride to his small church, which didn't turn out to be that small after all, took about ten minutes, and he talked all the way there.

He pointed out this building and that one, this place of business and those over there. Karl was excited, and even "hyper"; and they doubted that it was just about them. No, something else had this man burning on all twelve plugs and it had to be good. Both Tom and Jill wanted to ask, but didn't. By the time they arrived at his church, they felt like tourists on a guided tour. As they entered the building, the unmistakable smell of fresh pine greeted them.

"The Golden Years Class is downstairs making Christmas wreaths for this year's Christmas bazaar. That's why the pine smell," Karl explained.

"Smells fresh," Jill replied as Tom nodded in agreement.

"Yes it does," Karl answered, walking ahead of them.

As they entered the sanctuary, both Jill and Tom were struck with its simple elegance and beauty.

"This is beautiful Karl...Rev. Watts," Tom said.

"Thanks. It was already built by the time I got here, but you're right, it is beautiful. Just call me Karl, every one else does," he added.

"Reverend Watts," they all heard from the other end of the Sanctuary. As they turned they saw, strutting up the aisle like a peacock, Bill Bright Junior.

Karl couldn't keep from smiling. This young man could enter a room and bring smiles to everyone's face. He was full of life and you couldn't be around him for long without catching his spirit. Karl intended to introduce Bill Junior to the Smiths when he got closer, but half wayup the aisle he yelled,

"Hi! I'm Bill Jr., what's your names?"

By the time his self-introduction was complete Bill Jr. was close enough for Jill to answer,

"Jill and Tom Smith"

"Well, good to meet you, Jill and Tom Smith," Bill Junior said.

"Are you gonna join the Church?" he asked next.

"Well, I, that is...we were..."

"They're thinking about it, Bill Junior," Karl spoke up rescuing Jill.

"Coming to my Baptism tomorrow?" Bill Junior asked next.

"Well, I'm...we..we don't know."

"Think they should, Bill Junior?" Karl asked, knowing they would all be in for a short sermon from Bill Junior himself.

"Yes," he said emphatically.

"Baptism is a sacred act. It confirms, once and for all that you are a child of God. Right Reverend Watts?"

"Right, Bill Junior."

"And that's not all. Baptism...," and off he went. Bill Junior had studied the small book Karl had given him from cover to cover. He probably had it memorized, and without question understood the basic premise of Baptism. Karl had spent at least an hour with him each Saturday afternoon for the last six months Bill Junior was ready to be baptized.

"Isn't that right, Reverend Watts?"

"I think you've covered most of it Bill Junior," Karl answered.

"Well, you coming tomorrow?" Bill Jr. persisted.

"We'll try and make it, just for you Bill Jr," Tom said as shook the special young man's outstretched hand.

Jill and Tom's two children, guided by one of the Golden Years Class members, had found their way to the Preschool Department downstairs, next to the fellowship hall's pine wreaths activity. By the time Tom and Jill arrived, they were both eating a snack and being watched over by three of the Class members. It was obvious their children were eating up the attention.

"Such lovely children," One of the silver haried ladies said.

"Are you new in town?" asked another.

"Yes, we are," Jill said cautiously, wondering if these three fine ladies would be that nice to their kids if the truth was known.

"Do you live around here?" the first one asked.

"No. Well, we don't know yet," Jill corrected herself.

"We're looking," Tom added, knowing the truth would eventually come out if they stayed around here too long.

"Your children are having fun and they're in safe hands with us," the third member said. "Are you two doing something with Karl?" She continued.

"Yes," Tom said quickly, to cut off their inquiries. "Right now, though, he's practicing with Bill Jr."

All three ladies smiled at the report and accepted it as information from an 'almost one of them' couple. And the questioning stopped.

"Well, I see you found the kids," Karl said as he entered the room. "They're in good hands with these three," he added.

"Get Bill Jr. taken care of?" the silver head lady asked

"Yes, he's in good shape...Ready. He'll probably stay awake tonight and read his instruction manual through again," Karl added, and they all chuckled at the thought.

Karl could see that Jill and Tom were nervous. They had probably been bombarded with questions from these three ladies. He knew that it wasn't just prying on their part. You had to know about a person before you could help that person. You had to know about a couple before you could help that couple. He had been preaching concern for others for the last two years here. Concern for others could turn into prying, if you didn't watch. He could tell that Tom and Jill were wondering and worrying about the truth.

"Would you two like to join us in the Sanctuary? The kids are fine here," Karl added.

"Go on," one of the ladies said, "They'll be fine."

And so, without too much coaching, Tom and Jill followed Karl back up the stairs they had descended a half-hour earlier when Karl had started rehearsing with Bill Jr.

At the top of the stairs, Karl stopped and said to them,

"They mean well, you know. Hope they didn't put you through the wringer?"

"Nah not really," Tom said.

"But it was getting close," Jill added.

As the three of them entered the Sanctuary, Karl turned to Tom and Jill and said softly, "Bill Jr. has something to ask you. That's his father sitting in the pew." Bill Sr., with a smile on his face, acknowledged the long distance introduction with the nod of his head and the wave of a couple fingers.

"Hi, Tom and Jill," Bill Jr. said, as the three of them approached. "Listen," he continued as they walked closer. "Mom and Dad are throwing a party for me tonight at our place to celebrate my Baptism. Wanna come?"

Neither Tom nor Jill knew exactly what to say. This entire day had been Karl's idea. They had agreed to meet him at the buss stop because there wasn't any place else to go. Now here was this young man inviting them over to his parent's house for a...

"Just say yes," Karl said.

Tom and Jill both glanced over at the pew where Bill Jr.'s father was sitting, only to see him nodding his head and mouthing, "Yes". So they said, "Yes" While wondering and worrying about the truth.

"Great! See you there," Bill Jr. said as he walked, or better said, bounced down the aisle and out the front door of the church.

Karl broke the silence by leading the two over to the pew and saying,

"Now let me formally introduce you. Tom and Jill Smith, meet Bill Bright Sr."

Bill Sr. stood and shook hands with both of them as they exchanged greetings.

"Let's sit down here for a minute," Karl said.

"Bill?" he added as they took their seats and he nodded in Bill Sr.'s direction.

Bill Sr. picked up his cue and said,

"Karl here tells me you're new in town and need a place to stay, 'til you get yourselves situated and all. Well, we have this place I built for Bill Jr. a few years back. Sort of an 'in-law suite' you might say. He doesn't like it. Won't stay in it. Separate building in our back yard. Not much, mind you, but it has a nice sized living room in it, a big bedroom, and den we could make into a second bedroom for your kids, and a big bath. Lots of storage space for your stuff, and it might just do for a while. Wanna' take a look at it?"

Tom and Jill were dumbfounded. Where did this kind of generosity come from? Not from just going to church. They both knew 'good church going people.' They both had experience with 'good Christian folk' before. They both knew the viciousness and cruelty that could come from such people. In the business world, the word was out. It was precisely these kinds of people you watched out for. They would cheat you in a minute, steal your commissions in a second, stick a knife in your back without giving it a second thought. The church was not paradise, but a Pandora's box of people, many looking for someone to use as a pin cushion for their pent up emotions. They knew personally the pain of non-acceptance and final rejection. No, this generosity didn't come from church membership; it came from somewhere else. Or, was this the beginning of a short journey down a road that would lead, once again, into the pain of being outcasts? And if Karl had told him that much about them, what else had he, 'shared' with Bill Sr. and God knows how many others? Was betrayal part of his game? Had he spread 'the word' about their predicament before their arrival? Suspicion surrounded them both, fear of the truth being revealed squeezed unmercifully at their hearts and foreboding poured down on them like the darkest night. So this was Karl's game after all.

"OH, NO!" Karl yelled, shaking them from their thoughts of doom.

"NO, NO, NO, NO, NO!" he yelled again, startling them and Bill Sr.

"I know what your thinking. I don't know how, but I know what your thinking and It's not true! It's not true! I would never betray a trust! I would never, never, never". And hurt filled the eyes of Karl Watts. "Listen", he went on, desperate to explain.

"I knew that Bill Sr. had this place and I just asked him if you could use it for a while. That's all! That's all!"

"That's right," Bill Sr. said, looking first at Karl and then at them, with a frown on his face, wondering what was going on.

"Is there something here I should know about Reverend?" Bill Sr. asked. "I'm opening my home up here. Something else?" he asked.

And there it was. That space.

that awful space. That space once again where truth was to fit. They had been to this place before. This place where that space appeared, and they knew what was coming. They knew. And they, apparently had opened the space up, themselves. By their own actions and fears of rejection, they had just opened the space, and now the truth would come out, and they would have to leave, once again. The day had gone so well. Their crystal hopes, shattered, by their own hands.

"Last Sunday," Jill said, her eyes glazed over in a daze as she stared at the cross above the altar,

"Last Sunday...morning, we left the shelter we were staying at, took the kids and went to church. It wasn't a good experience. It was a mistake. As soon as we walked through the front doors of the Church, we knew we had made a mistake. Oh, they handed us bulletins, but they didn't smile. They didn't say, "Welcome". They didn't want us. There were frowns and questionable looks. The kids were taken to Sunday School Class but afterwards, on the way back to the shelter, the kids said they didn't feel comfortable. It's hard to fool children you know. For the most part, they just pretended we were not even there, and no one shook our hands or touched our shoulders, not even the kids. Not even when, in the middle of the worship service, they shared the peace of Jesus Christ. No one shared the peace with us. No one spoke. And when we left, no one said, "Come back, not even the minister." Jill looked Karl Watts straight in the face, and continued,

"Guess people know when you have the virus, whether rather you tell them or not."

and the truth was revealed. That space had been filled. ...and here they were, once again, at that place.

"Listen, there's a lot of bad people in the world, and some of them go to church," Bill Sr. said.

"But not all churchgoing people are bad people," he continued.

"A lot of churchgoing people are good people. Reverend Watts here didn't tell me a thing about your physical problems. He just told me you' needed a place to stay 'til you got situated. That's all. Sounds to me like that's still the case, isn't it? I know what it's like to be rejected. I know what it's like to have your child rejected. I know the c Church or some churches I should say, don't want certain people. My wife and I experienced the same feelings years ago with Bill Jr. you're expressing here today. We've been there, where you are, and we know the pain. So you just bundle yourselves up and come home with me. My wife and I won't have all the answers, but we'd like to try and help. Wha-da-ya-say?"

Tom and Jill's emotions were like a rollercoster right then. They felt terrible after accusing Karl and relieved that he had not broken their trust. They felt hope with Bill Sr. when he invited them to his home even after the truth had been revealed. How could they apologize? How could they accept? How were they to proceed?

"Come on", Bill Sr. said, as he stood up. "Lets go home."

As Tom and Jill stood with him, they looked at Karl and felt terrible.

"Don't worry about it," Karl said. "Hope to see you in church tomorrow morning for Bill Junior's Baptism."

"Oh, we'll be there...here for sure..Karl...Reverend Watts." Jill said.

Karl didn't correct her, this time, for calling him Reverend. He knew it was her way of saying; "We're sorry for thinking the worse of you." He made a point to walk to the end of the pew as they were exiting and gave each of them one of his famous hugs.

Tony pulled all the information available on drifters, homeless, shelter, food kitchen and all the other possibilities. Problem was, these people didn't leave records and those helping them didn't keep good records either. His list was short and, he knew, inadequate. None of the information on hand led him to believe any of these men were the mysterious stalker of the new family in town. But he knew that didn't matter. You could have all the resources in the world but if a man wanted to do something, he could do it. Stalk a family in his town or any? Of course. So he planned to keep a closer eye on the new waitress down at Shelley's Restaurant, and her two kids as well.

It didn't dawn on Terry 'til later, a couple hours later. They were still riding around in Jerrey's not- so "beautiful car", when it dawned on him. Tony had to have a pretty good idea who the girl was, and where she lived. A family, regardless of how small, couldn't move into downtown without Tony knowing it. He knew the downtown like the back of his hand and watched it even closer. If he knew where the small family lived, then he'd keep an eye on them. Tony wouldn't want anything bad to happen downtown that he could prevent. No, he knew who they were and where they were living, Terry was sure of it, but he wasn't going to say anything to Jerrey. Not now. Not now...and Terry looked out his side window and smiled. Tony would keep and eye on them.

"Jerrey, we need to call it a day," Terry said.
"One more time around town," Jerrey offered.
"No, lets call it a day. Besides it's getting late and we have to be at my house in an hour and a half. You have to go

home and clean up. By the way, take a shower will you? Take me back to my car."

"I have to clean up to come over to your place?" Jerrey joked. "Forget it. I'm not coming," he went on.

"Right," Terry responded.

As Terry exited Jerrey's car and entered his own, parked in front of Shelley's, a curtain on the second floor slide back so the occupant of Shelley's old apartment could see what was going on down on the street below.

"There's that jerk and his friend ," Ashley thought. "Banged-up car and all. Good. Hope he has a flat tire or something on the way home," she thought as she walked away from the window and the curtain closed behind her.

Terry saw the curtain close and knew some one was living now in Shelley's old apartment. When he spotted Tony sitting in his patrol car a half-block away, he put it together. They had been driving around all day searching for a family that had been right under their noses. As Jerrey drove away, Terry hesitated for a minute. It didn't take long. Tony pulled his patrol car up beside Terry and rolled down his window.

"I'll keep and eye on things, counselor," Tony said.

Terry nodded as he said, "Know you will Tony Evenin' now"

"Evening," Tony answered

Terry eased his sports car out onto the street and headed for home.

Ashley watched the jerk and his friend leave and then went back to getting ready. For, upstairs in the apartment, the Smith-Broden family was getting ready to go out. Shelley had been invited to a party or something and had mentioned them to the family throwing the party; and the family had, 'insisted.' Shelley said, that they come along. Something about their son being baptized tomorrow and such. Neither Katherine nor Ashley had heard of throwing a party for a Baptism, but what the heck...a chance to get out and meet some people, and on a Saturday night at that. Why not? They had agreed. When Katherine had mentioned Sammy,

Shelley said she had already brought that up and there would be other kids there his age.

Katherine didn't have much to wear but it was clean. Ashley had washed everything they had that morning. Well, it was cleanliness that was next to Godliness anyway wasn't it?

Chapter Eleven
PREPARATION PARTIES

Evelyn arrived home exhausted. She had doubled again the number of presents she had purchased by noon that day, and subsequently the number of boxes. She laughed to herself as she thought "I wonder what Terry would have said if he had seen me with all the additional boxes since this morning?" Well, everyone laughed at her now, but they wouldn't be laughing Christmas morning. No, on Christmas morning they would all appreciate her shopping efforts. On this, she was sure.

Evelyn was fully aware that the kids were grown. In fact, everyone else she bought presents for was grown as well. But that didn't matter. It didn't dampen Evelyn's Christmas spirit one iota. She bought presents and hid the boxes in her's and Ted's bedroom: under the bed, in the closet, and anywhere else she needed to. She refused to allow anyone to sneak a peek or open a present early. Christmas Eve, right before church, was the time the family gathered and opened presents and not before. It had been a tradition in the family since, well, since she had married Ted. His family had the tradition going before she married him. She had just taken it up and carried it forward. Now it was a family tradition and that's the way it was-and it wasn't going to change she hoped. Evelyn didn't like changes, especially when change eliminated a tradition. She had grown up with many family traditions in Louisville, the family tradition of having breakfast and dinner together each day. The family tradition of inviting a family over for lunch on Sundays after church services, the family tradition of Christmas Eve, when the pastor and his wife and family were always invited over after the Christmas Eve service, and a few other traditions she loved.

Ted had brought her here to meet his mother and Mary shortly after his discharge from the Army. They had not married yet. Though Ted had asked her and she had said yes, Ted wanted his Mother and Mary's approval. She would never forget that weekend. Mary had greeted her with open arms and had accepted Evelyn even before she met her. "If Teddy's in love with you, honey," Mary had said, "then that's all that matters." Mary had helped to make that weekend tolerable. But Ted's mother was a different story all together.

Evelyn could tell that Ted's mother was passing judgement on every move she made that weekend. Oh, she was cordial, kind, and polite, and a true lady; but she was sizing Evelyn up. Evelyn knew what she was thinking the entire weekend: "Is this girl good enough for my Teddy?" Part of Evelyn wanted to tell Ted's mother to go jump in a lake, but the other part understood his mother's concern. After all, Ted was all she had left of a marriage. Ted had told Evelyn as much about his father's disappearance as he could remember. Evelyn was glad that he had. It helped to explain and understand his mother's concern for her only child.

Evelyn swallowed hard several times that weekend. In the end, Ted's mother, along with Mary, gave her support to their marital plans but had insisted they come and live on the ranch. At first Ted didn't want to, but Evelyn had convinced him that it would be a wonderful place to raise children and she could handle any intrusion into their family matters by his mother or Mary.

"Remember what it was like growing up as a little boy on a ranch, Ted?" had been Evelyn's deciding question. Ted's answer eliminated all resistance in his mind. After the wedding, they honeymooned in Acapulco Mexico and then returned to the ranch, thirty-three years ago next month.

"Mary, where's Grandma?" Evelyn asked, as she walked into kitchen.

"Grandma wasn't feeling too well Miss Evelyn, so she went in to lie down for a few minutes."

"How long's that been now?" Evelyn asked.

"'Bout half an hour ago."

"I'm going to check on her." Evelyn said as she walked out of the kitchen and down the hall.

At the bottom of the steps, she picked up a few items left there by various members of the family and carried them up the stairs with her, depositing them on the second floor where she thought they belonged. The door to Grandma's bedroom was slightly open, so Evelyn peeked in, expecting to see Grandma lying asleep oh her bed. Instead, she gasped, and realizing the noise she had just made in doing so, put her hand to her mouth to cover...but it was too late. Grandma, standing in front of her full length swivel mirror, was naked as a jay bird. When Grandma heard Evelyn's gasp, she turned, startled that someone had seen her.

"Grandma?" Evelyn asked as she entered the bedroom and closed the door behind her, "Are you all right?"

Grandma just smiled and said,

"You know, when I was a little girl, Sunny Thomason told me that I was so cute. And that I was going to grow up and have a lot of cute dimples. Now Evelyn, I'm eighty one years old, and I've been looking at my body and all these dimples...and they don't look so cute to me."

Evelyn burst into laughter with Grandma as they both reached for Grandma's gown.

"Here Grandma, put this on before you scare the birds" Evelyn said, as they both laughed even harder. After the two women calmed down somewhat, but still chuckling, Grandma said,

"You know Evelyn, I don't know if I've ever told you before, but you know I love you."

And time paused for a moment in Grandma's upstairs bedroom.

No, she didn't know that. Or at least, she had never heard that before, not out loud. Not from the mouth of this lady. She had married Ted and moved in years earlier. She and

Ted had raised a family here. They had lived together for years in the same house. She had thought at times that Grandma might love her, and then there were those times when she was convinced the opposite was true. Certainly, over the years, they had been cordial to one another. They had shared the children and the rest of the family together. They had counted on each other. They had helped each other. But not until now, not until this very moment had she ever heard Grandma say: "Evelyn, you know I love you" And the words wiped Evelyn's plate clean. All the times in the past, when she had wanted to tell Ted's mother how much she loved her, came rushing forward. All the times when she wanted to put her arms around this lady and thank her for just being there blew gently, like a cool wind against Evelyn's soul and she said, without containing her emotion successfully,

"I love you too, Grandma. Can I give you a hug?"

"Well, of course you can give me a hug, Evelyn." Grandma walked over to her daughter-in-law and, in the upstairs bedroom of the oldest, the two ladies of the house embraced one another...for the first time...for the first time...and but for a moment the pause continued...this time for each.

"Well," Grandma said, as the embrace ended, "we'd better get ready before our guests arrive. What do you think?" she asked, as she walked over to her ottoman and took out the pale blue dress hanging there, and swung it around for Evelyn to see.

"That will be perfect," Evelyn said, composing herself and readjusting to time.

"I haven't worn this old dress in years, but it still fits," Grandma said.

"I tried it on the other night and, to my surprise, I still looked good in it. And it covered up all the dimples, too."

Evelyn's smile was back.

"Evelyn, can we talk about something for a minute?" Grandma asked as she proceeded to lay out her clothes for the evening on her bed.

"Sure," Evelyn said, wondering what was next.

"We both know my time is coming...and I'm ready for it. I'm tired and I'm worn out. I've lived a good life. Had a lot of fun. Raised Teddy as best I knew how. Carried on after his Daddy disappeared. Kept this place up, as best I could. You and Ted have surely helped in more ways then one. You both have made my life these past few years a real joy, living with you here and watching your kids grow up. Evelyn, it might sound silly and selfish on my part. It might be pure nonsense but, after I'm gone, after I'm gone..." and Grandma hesitated as she had done so many times over the years. Evelyn knew from experience with her that if she didn't speak up now Ted's mother would not finish her sentence. She would just swallow the thought as she had done so many times before over the years.

"Go on Grandma," Evelyn encouraged "Just you and me here, go on."

"It would mean so much to me, for you and Teddy and your children...it's meant so much to me, that you...that we all met on the Verandah late every afternoon as a family and had that time together. Do you think, Evelyn, that you'll continue doing that after I'm gone?" And Evelyn knew the mind of her mother-in law even better.

"Grandma, you know we will continue to meet on the Verandah. You and Grandpa started a family tradition that will last for generations. We wouldn't think of stopping it."

Ted had grown up in this house he was looking at. He could barely remember his Daddy. Didn't remember the last day when his Daddy told his mother and Mary that he would be gone for a while. But he did remember him, somewhat. He couldn't remember the sound of his voice, but when he looked at pictures of himself as a little boy with his Daddy, then he remembered. They were good memories, what he could remember, and that wasn't much. He did remember being on the Verandah with him, playing in the back yard and a horseback ride. He vaguely remembered riding in the car with him once. That was about it.

Ted had grown up with his mother and Mary looking after his every need. "Let's not spoil him." If he heard it once he heard a thousand times from each of them. And while they both said it, both ignored it. Ted thought he had been spoiled rotten. But wasn't that to be expected from the parent or parents of an only son? Grade school through high school, spoiled rotten. But, in the long run, he had turned out okay. At least Evelyn thought so.

Standing on the back porch looking out over the field toward the tree line, Ted was sure what made him turn out "Okay" was his military experience, especially Fort Knox. For it was while he was in basic training at Fort Knox that he met the Louisville beauty, Evelyn Kinker. Every time the radio played one of those early sixties songs, the ones he and his buddies in the army always listened to while in basic training, his mind flashed back to days gone by. And the older he got, the more he wished he could go back, to a few of them anyway, like the weekend when he had met Evelyn.

Basic training was coming to and end. Three-day passes were being handed out and Louisville, some forty miles away was their destination. More specifically, the Brown Hotel in downtown Louisville. Two of them had checked in and paid for double occupancy in the room, but as soon as Ted and one of his buddies checked in, six more of their buddies joined them. Eight in a room made the Brown Hotel very affordable for the weekend.

They had walked Fourth Street, the busiest strip with the most bars on it, stopping in each for a drink or two of course. When the routine became a bore. Someone said the Y.W.C.A. was where the U.S.O. was, and there would be a dance there later. It didn't take long to find it on Fifth Street.

Ted had been surprised at all the food that was being provided free by one of the local churches. He was even more surprised at the size of the band playing and the guys and girls already dancing by the time they arrived. Most of the evening he sat drinking coke, (no booze allowed), and eating one homemade sandwich after the other. That is, until he spotted Evelyn dancing with another Private First Class.

As in one of the songs of the day, "She was a dark haired beauty." She wore a black dress with a low scoop neckline that pointed out all of her beauty and high-lighted her gorgeous face. Her shoulder length hair cushioned around her face softened, even more so, her Southern persona. He watched her and watched her, until he was forced by his own desire to meet her, to rise and walk over to where she was sitting.

He waited 'til one of the numbers being played by the band came to its conclusion and then he headed her way. Just as the Private First Class walked away from where she was sitting, after thanking her for the dance, Ted approached her. "Good evening," he had said. Ted could remember as though it was yesterday. She looked up at him, smiled the most beautiful smile he had ever seen and said to him, "Good evening, soldier." Her beauty, smile, and Southern draw melted Teddy Habersham right there and then. He knew-he didn't know how he would work it out, he didn't know anything about her-but he knew this was his woman, his woman forever.

When the music started up again Ted, still standing there looking at her in amazement, asked her to dance. She accepted, and that was that. He had met Evelyn at a U.S.O. dance. The church providing the food for the soldiers that evening was her church, Third Lutheran Church of Louisville, KY...and Ted had thanked that church in his mind since.

As she pulled into the driveway, Betsy's eyes caught the beauty of the old place once again. The old house was still a magnificent structure. Not huge in comparison to some of the houses they were building today, but solid. Laid out on the land in a beautiful manner, as though it had grown up from the grounds like the trees that surrounded it...and the trees, side by side an yet each separate and wonderful to behold. It was as though a master architect, builder, or craftsman had constructed this place and had it laid out by a landscape artist, who decided to bring all his artistic abilities to focus on one place. This place...Grandpa's place. Grandma's place. The place where she was blessed to live, for now.

She wondered what would happen to the old place when her Grandma passed on. Would her folks sell it or continue to live here? Would she and her sister and brother inherit it? As Betsy pulled her car into its usual place and turned off the engine, she took a moment or two to reflect on her own thoughts. *She did love this place,* she thought, *more than most.*

Startled when the door to her car opened, she shook her hand just enough to spill the contents of a paper cup over her hand and down on her skirt.

"Didn't mean to scare you honey," her dad said, standing there, guilty of the deed, holding her door open.

"Just wanted to be a gentleman," he added.

"You didn't do anything Dad, I spilled the stuff."

"Well, I just couldn't stand to see a pretty lady, even if she is a doctor, just sitting here. Penny for your thoughts?" Ted asked.

"Oh, I was just thinking how much I love this place Dad."

"Know what you mean honey. I love it too."

"What would Grandpa say, if he could see it now?" she asked.

"Hard to say. I think he would love it. After all, it's been kept up pretty well, don't you think?" Ted asked.

"You and Mom have done a great job keeping it up Dad."

"Thanks. May I escort you into our home, Doctor Habersham."

"You may, Mr. Habersham, sir."

And the man standing out by the fence in the dark brown over coat, with a bright red scarf thrown around his neck, watched as father and daughter walked hand in arm together, into the house.

"What happened to your car Jerrey?" his mother asked as the three of them walked out of their home.

"Nothing. Nothing. Just hit something. It will be fixed," Jerrey answered.

"You're not hurt or anything are you?" She continued.

"No Mom, I'm not hurt or anything. Everything's fine. The car will be fixed and everything will be okay."

"Was anyone else hurt?" she persisted, as she slid into the front passengers seat of his dad's car.

"No Mom. No one was hurt," Jerrey added as he looked over the top of the car to see his dad smiling at him in that knowing 'mothers will be mothers,' smile.

"Well, how much will it cost to get your car fixed?" his mother went on, as his father pulled the car out of the driveway.

"George said he could fix it for about two hundred to two-fifty," Jerrey answered, tired of the inquisition.

"Well, that's not too bad, is it Bud?" his mother asked his father.

"No, that's pretty good as a matter of fact. Jerrey, you're sure no one was hurt?" his Dad asked, while smirking at his son in the mirror.

"Yes, I'm sure Dad," Jerrey answered, thinking fast.

"Dad," Jerrey asked, "are we going to Florida again this year for Christmas?" and the dig was returned with equal force.

Christmas in Florida had been his Dad's dream for years. He had talked about it and planned for it, but no one wanted to go. After a decade of talking it up and planning for it, the family had given in to his Dad's dream, just this last Christmas as a matter of fact, and they had all gone to Florida. It rained the entire week they were down there, while the weather around their home had been beautiful. Three of the grandchildren had taken ill and half the presents were stolen from Mark's van. It was not a fun time. The entire family had harassed Jerrey's Dad since.

"I doubt it," his Dad answered, and the three of them smiled as they looked out separate windows.

Bill Junior answered the door again. This time it was Shelley with some other people.

"Come in" Bill Junior said to all of them.

"Bill Junior this is Katherine, Ashley, and Sammy Smith," Shelley said as she led the small group into the foyer.

"Glad to meet you," Bill Junior said, as he helped with their coats.

"Come on in an meet everyone," he continued as he walked into the living room.

"Everyone, this is Shelley, Katherine, Ashley and Sammy," Bill Junior repeated, proud of his ability to remember names.

Everyone greeted and welcomed them as though they were old friends.

"Welcome," a well-dressed lady said as she approached them. "I'm Bill Junior's mother. How about something to eat?" she said as she encouraged the three of them over to her dining room table, heaped high with food.

The entire house, downstairs and upstairs, was filled with people. Some were eating and drinking, finding it challenging to balance their drinks and small plates of food while standing, others meeting the challenge of talking with a mouth full of food. While yet others were seemingly content to simply be caught up in conversation.

"Shelley," Bill Junior's mother said,

"I must confess, I haven't had one of your famous cinnamon rolls in months, and I'm dying to have one."

"I'll have one waiting for you tomorrow morning," Shelley said. "Bring Bill Junior down before you go to church and I'll treat him. It'll be my Baptism present to him," Shelley continued.

"Well now, we just might do that," Bill Junior's mother added, accepting the invitation.

"Ashley, it is Ashley isn't it?" she asked.

"Yes ma'am, it is." Ashley answered, remembering her upbringing.

"Do you like sugar-cured ham?"

"Well, what do you think?" Bill Sr. asked in a hush voice.

"We think it will do just fine." Jill answered quietly as Tom, standing beside her, nodded.

"Great then. It's settled," Bill Senior said, "It's yours as long as you want it. Enjoy the party. Get something to eat," he added as he walked over to greet another couple.

It had been easier then expected, walking into Bill Senior's house. People were arriving already for Bill Junior's Baptism party. Bill Senior had even introduced them to a few couples as they journeyed through the front door of his home and out the back. With everyone else arriving, it looked as though they were just arriving for Bill Junior's party as well.

There in the back yard was a freshly painted, quaint little coach house, built especially for, but rejected by, Bill Junior. The quarter-acre courtyard created naturally by the two buildings was filled with flowers around a central fountain. Red brick walkways weaved between the two as shade trees, and kept the breeze blowing cooler than out front. Once inside the coach house, Jill and Tom could see no detail had been forgotten or left out. The small building, immaculate and well maintained on the outside, was warm and rich with colors on the inside. Why Bill Jr. had rejected the idea of living here in 'his own place', no one knew. But then again, no one had pressed him, in order to ask. If he wanted to live here fine. If not, fine. But his rejections made it available to Tom and Jill.

"Look around and think it over," Bill Senior had said.

"Come on back into the party when you're ready. Oh, by the way, if you want to freshen up, the water and everything's working," he added as he walked out the front door of the coach house back toward the back of the main house, and into the growing party.

Gwen had been distraught all afternoon. The luncheon revelation had burst her plans. The balloon she had slowly inflated over the past year had exploded in front of her face and sent her emotions flying this way and that. By the time she made it back to her perfumery, she was an emotional wreck. But business was business and that even included men business. If he wasn't for her, then he wasn't for her and that was that, or at least that's what she kept telling herself all afternoon. Accomplishing little, she left the business in the able hands of her employees and headed home a half-hour early.

To relieve her frustration and calm her anxiety-after all there were guests coming over to the house this evening-she decided to take an alternative route home. Truth was, it wasn't an alternate route at all but an excuse she used occasionally to help eliminate her growing frustration over the entire mess,

the entire mess of her life. It was a mess because while she could do some things right, like her business, she couldn't do the most important thing right, like find the right man. And finding the right man was the most important thing to Gwen.

By the time she shifted her sports car into fifth gear, the car was already traveling ninety miles an hour. Fifth gear took it to over a hundred in seconds. On a small country road, at a hundred miles and hour, trees fly by. Fence posts run together, inches apart, and one can experience the temporary feeling of leaving all life's problems behind. At that speed, the only exception is the problem that lies ahead. And what lay ahead for Gwen was a problem.

As she masterfully steered her little sports car around a slow bend in the road, now easing up past one hundred and ten miles an hour, the wind rushing by her as she cut a wedge in the thick late afternoon air, not more then a half mile ahead of her: a doe-A DEER!-A DEER!...stepped out onto the blacktop road. Her reflexes, slowed somewhat by her afternoon ordeal, sparked into action. But it would be too late, and she knew it. She would never stop in time before hitting the deer and at this speed they would probably both be killed.

Was this the way it was to end? Was this, by her own hand, by her own doing, by her own silly, reckless behavior, going to be it? Was her life to be nothing more than a perfumery and a sports car? Was this going to be it? Smashed up against a deer that had no business being out on the highway this time of day in the first place.

She threw the car into third gear, popped the clutch and stepped on the brake petal hard as she dared without throwing herself into a spin. The front of her car nosed downward, inched from the blacktop. Her peripheral vision caught sight of a pickup truck on her left, as it's driver eased the front end out onto the highway, stopping abruptly as he saw her approach.

Just beyond the pickup was a man dressed in something dark with something red around his neck - he was pointing across the street.

She looked across the street just in time to see the gravel road angled off to her right, and eased her sports car onto it. The forward momentum of the car shot her up the gravel road but the gravel refused to accept her braking tires and threw her into a slow forward spin, whipping the car off the gravel and onto a high grass field littered with fully grown pine trees and oaks. The grass slowed her momentum but not enough. Her car barely missed a hung oak and was headed straight for a pine tree when the car's rear axle gave way spreading the car's tires outward and whipping her back the other way and onto the softball field which lay next to the high grass field. When the car finally stopped, Gwen was sitting in the middle of the softball diamond, all alone, engulfed in a cloud of dust and smoke. But she was stopped, and still alive.

Gwen sat there, in the middle of the softball diamondwith her cars axle broken, as the pick-up pulled up and stopped on the gravel road. The driver got out and yelled, "You okay?" But Gwen couldn't answer. She couldn't move. The shock of the incident had numbed her brain, or so it seemed. She didn't know, but she couldn't move. Her mouth was dry and she began to shiver, as though it was winter. Then she had to get out. She had to run. Run away from what had just happened. She pushed and pulled herself up out of the broken car and began to run across the softball diamond. Only when the truck driver grabbed her and held her tight, so she couldn't run, did she stop. Her mind was a blur and the instant replay wouldn't stop. Minutes passed. Then, finall,y still holding her tight in his arms, the truck driver eased his hold on her, and she moved slowly back to the moment, and reality.

"Oh, my God," was all that Gwen could say before breaking down in tears "Oh, my God", she said over and over and over.

Red and blue spinning lights atop four door sedans arrived one by one, and Gwen was seated gently in the back seat of one of them. Over the next forty-five minutes the deputies, with the aid of the truck driver, pieced together the replay of the incident while Gwen, wrapped in a warm blanket, rested.

"Miss, again, I think it would be best if you'd let us drive you by the hospital and let them take a look at you," the deputy said.

"No, I'll be fine. I'll be fine," she replied.

"We've called George's garage for a tow truck.

They should be here soon," the deputy went on.

"Thank you."

"Now we'll take you where ever you want to go. Where would that be Miss?

"Home...if someone could drive me home," Gwen answered.

"Sure enough Miss, I'll get someone." And the Deputy walked away from the still stunned lady.

"Gwen, I'll drive you home. Come on", Joe said as he reached into the back seat of the car to help her out.

Joe Wilder had been an old flame of Gwen's in high school. Nothing serious or anything. They both knew, at the time, they were just dating. She had already planned on opening the perfumery, downtown, and he had planned on going away to college. Both had followed their plans, or at least part of them. She had also planned on having a family. He had also planned on graduating. Neither had fulfilled all their dreams: Well, not yet anyway. Joe had arrived back in town just two years after going away and had joined the Sheriff's Department almost immediately. The old high school grapevine, kept up and running by some of her old schoolmates, had informed her the day Joe had started dating Kim Paxton. That had been all right with Gwen, She had her business to take care of right then. She wished them well, meant it, and told them both at their wedding. Now Joe was going to drive her home.

As they slid into the front seat of his patrol car, George's tow truck drove away with her once-beautiful car. After maneuvering the patrol car around the field, up over the rut-marked grass and gravel, and up onto the blacktop, Joe stopped and said,

"Gwen, do you still live out on the ranch?"

"Still live out on the ranch," she said, wondering if he thought she shouldn't be.

Joe turned right and headed towards the ranch. They had only driven a couple miles when he looked over at her and knew exactly what she was doing. It always happened; he had seen it a hundred times. Trauma has a way of coming back on people. It replayed itself over and over in the mind. And if you let it, it will drive you mad.

"Stop it," he said, breaking the silence.

"Stop it?" she answered. "Stop what?"

"Stop thinking about it. It's over. No one was hurt and it's over. Let it go. Won't do you any good thinking about it. Thank God you're alive and no one was hurt…and let it go."

Gwen had no response. She knew he was right.

"By the way, still like Lilac don't you?" And they both laughed. Her use of Lilac, even in high school, had generated some classroom talk.

"How's business?" he asked.

"Doing well," she answered. "How's the family?"

"Well," Joe said, "that's another subject."

"Oh?" Gwen asked, deciding to use one of Betsy's old tricks. "Tell me about it."

"Another time maybe," he said, as he pulled the patrol car into the driveway of the Habersham ranch. "Right now, Gwen, you need some rest."

He offered to help her into the house, but she refused his polite and concerned offer, and waved to him as he eased out of the driveway and back onto the main road.

Gwen walked slowly and quietly into the house and up to her second floor bedroom. She was sure that a good cry and an hour or so rest would calm her nerves and ease the hurt away. She just made it to her bedroom in time. The tears wouldn't wait.

An hour later, she seemed all cried out, but the hurt was still there. "Over a year...over a year," she said out loud and the tears started to flow again...into sleep.

As the late afternoon sun touched the tops of the tall pines in the far field, Mary found herself once again on the Verandah, alone.

She had started coming up here early, before set-up time, before Grandma, before the rest of the family, years earlier. It was her 'quiet time'. But now she knew it was more than just her quiet time. It was her 'Sanctuary.' She had found that out when her pastor had preached a powerful sermon one Sunday.   Sanctuary was a place you went in your spirit," he had said.   "A place where you leave all the troubles of your mind behind...a place where worry and fret were not allowed...a place where heart ache and heartbreak were released. A place where bad memories and bad deeds, mistakes, and guilt was dropped: never to be picked up again, For, in the midst of dropping them off your back, they would disappear forever." This was the time, and physical place, Mary had designated years earlier as her 'quiet time', her 'Sanctuary.' Though she had never really said that out loud to anyone. She didn't even know if anyone knew she came up here early and, if so, if they cared. Busy as they were, they probably didn't even know about it. That was fine with her. She looked forward to this time of the day, every day.

She walked, as usual, over to the banister and looked out over the grassy pasture at a mare and her fold playing in the tall grass. Rabbits? Why the back field was full of rabbits and she smiled to herself as they jumped everywhere she looked. A cool breeze announced evening's approach as she thought back over the day's activities. That's what Mary did when she came up here early. She thought back over the day's activities to count the blessings. Each day was full of blessings, she thought, you just had to stop and count them before you forgot them. Then Mary would plan for tomorrow. She would plan to look for tomorrow's blessings and catch them as they happened. For Mary, this was the best part of the day and the best place to be this time of every day.

"Oh..." she said out loud, as she stood there looking, "life can be so beautiful!"

But Mary hadn't grown up in a perfect world and she didn't live in fantasy land either, no-sir. While the Habershams had taken her in and treated her as well as anyone, like a member of the family, she knew, first-hand, that there was evil out there in the world. She had been witness to its chilling menace; and not only witness, but also victim to its conniving cruelty. Evil, she knew, didn't announce itself but rather slithered in like a snake in the night.

For Mary, there were those people who seemed to invite evil's promise-of victory over others-into their lives. They seemed to enjoy winning at the expense of others. They would gloat after successfully cheating someone. They would strut after crushing another human being. They would, sometimes even in the name of God, destroy another person. They could violate and rape, and brag about it. Mary knew, first-hand, some of these people. Then there were those that evil just used, temporarily, to carry out its will. Most of them didn't even know - were not even aware - of how evil was playing them like a sour flute, blowing evil's intentions in the face of what was right and good.

How could they know, if they never took time out of each day to look for God's blessings in their lives? For Mary knew that when you searched and discovered the blessings, you also unmasked evil's presence lurking in the shadows, waiting to destroy once again. Only when you could spot it and knew it was there could you name it, combat it, and call God to shoo it away.

No, Mary didn't live in a fantasy land, but she did live in a beautiful place with beautiful people, where she could experience 'Sanctuary.' As she stood there on the Verandah for another minute, in silence, Mary prepared for tomorrow's blessing.

"Grandma, you look beautiful," Betsy said as she walked down the upstairs hall towards her grandmother.
"Thank you, Thank you very much."
"Do you and Mary need some help setting up? I mean with the guests and all?" Betsy asked.
"No, thank you. We have it all taken care of. But why don't you get cleaned up and come over and talk to us before the others arrive?"
"I'll do that." Betsy said as her grandmother walked down the hall in the opposite direction. For a second, Betsy didn't know if Mary and her grandma needed help and didn't want to admit it or if her grandmother had felt herself rude for refusing Betsy's offer to help. Then, on second thought, she knew her grandma pretty well. That old lady would have spoken up if she needed help.

Terry was standing at the end of the driveway talking to another couple and their older son, when Karl and Alice drove up. Alice recognized both young men at once. The one was Betsy's brother, she couldn't remember his name, and the other one was the young man Betsy's brother was with yesterday when they almost bumped into each other outside Shelley's restaurant.
"The dark haired one is Betsy's younger brother." She told Karl as they drove up the drive. And the other guy is his friend. I don't know the couple with them. Probably Betsy's brother's friend."
Karl smiled and said, "I've met the two boys before."
"You have? When?" Alice asked between her teeth, with a smile on her face since they were getting so close to the others now.

"Its a long story. I'll tell you later," Karl said as he smiled back at her while the two boys starred at him from the driveway.

As they opened the car doors, the oldest of the four men extended his hand to Alice and helped her out of the car, saying,

"Good evening. My name is Burt Walker and this is my wife Nancy, and our son Jerrey."

While Alice shook hands with Nancy, Burt, always the ringmaster, continued,

"And I'm sure you know Terry Habersham?"

"Karl Watts, and my wife Alice," Karl said as he shook hands with Burt and Alice.

"Yes," he said gracefully, "Terry and I have met before," as he shook hands with him.

"Jerrey is it?" Karl said as he turned towards him, "Glad to see you again."

Alice thought she had missed something in the introductions but couldn't figure out what. As a mater of fact Burt and Nancy thought the same thing.

The moment's awkwardness was overpowered by the sudden and unmistakable smell of Lilac walking down the sidewalk in the form of one Gwen Habersham, who said as she approached, "Yo'al can come inside, you know."

"Gwen, you're even lovelier then the last time I saw you," Burt said as he approached her arms open, and gave her a peck on the cheek.

"Burt, you say that to all the women," She replied

"Besides Burt," Nancy said, as she and Gwen hugged each others shoulders, "she's way too young for you anyway."

As Nancy spoke, Gwen looked over at Karl and Alice and said,

"Hi, Mom and Dad."

Alice's face turned four shades of red all at once. What made it even worse was when everyone turned to look at Alice's face and guessed what Gwen had meant.

"You're pregnant?" Nancy asked Alice.

"Yes," is all Alice could manage to say in such an embarrassing moment.

"Congratulations!" Burt said as he smiled at Alice and shook Karl's hand so hard Karl looked at his red knuckles after the release.

Then they all chimed in, "Congratulations...when's it due..."

"Listen," Gwen said, proud of herself that she had managed to spill the beans so successfully,

"Let's continue this inside. What do you say?"

As she headed up the sidewalk toward the house, Burt escorting her while the others in conversation followed, Gwen was determined that someday she too would be the proud mother of a child and husband, too.

The conversation about Alice's pregnancy had just about died down, but Betsy revived it as they stepped out onto the Verandah.

"There's the prod Mommy," Betsy said, as she walked over to greet Alice.

"Karl, did you have anything to do with this?" Betsy went on.

Now it was Karl's turn to be a little embarrassed as he said, "Well, a little."

"Reverend. Watts, Alice, it's good to have you over. What would you like to drink? We have...." Ted said as he led the Watts family over to the beverage table.

Terry and Jerrey stood away from the rest of the crowd. After filling their glasses and small plates, they decided to walk down to the other end of the Verandah, look out over the field and talk about, The Man Who couldn't be caught.

"I don't know, Jerrey. You might have to give up the chase. Maybe he's left town by now," Terry said, with a mouth full of quiche.

"Maybe. But, I thought, well, I don't know. You know..."

Their 'deep thought,' philosophical conversation was interrupted by Jerrey's favorite teaser as she said,

"Evening, Jerrey."

"Evening Gwen," Jerry replied as a few drops of his drink spilled out his mouth and onto his open collar shirt.

"I didn't mean to make you slobber, Jerrey," Gwen said as she wiped the drops off his shirt with her napkin.

"You have that effect on him, sis. Every time you come around, he starts slobbering," Terry said, pleased with himself.

"Don't you listen to him Jerrey. He's just jealous." Gwen said, and then wondered herself what she meant by that.

"Jealous?" Terry asked.

"Yes, jealous that you don't have a women who likes to see you as much as I like to see Jerrey," Gwen said.

She didn't know where the thought came from that allowed her to come up with such a good answer, but she was thankful for it just the same.

"You look nice tonight Jerrey," she continued.

"Thanks," he replied.

"Yo'al need anything?" Terry asked, as he held up his empty glass.

"No, I'm okay," Jerrey said.

"No, thank you," Gwen said.

"Excuse me then," Terry said as he walked away from the two toward the refreshment table.

Terry noticed that everyone else was in one big group talking about, numerous subjects, including, Alice's baby, Betsy's practice, the family's ranch, some baptism Reverend Watts was going to do, and bragging about Grandma's food which she abruptly told them was Mary's doing. After he filled his glass and refilled his small plate, Terry intended to walk back over and join Gwen and Jerrey. But when he turned their way, he changed his mind. Jerrey didn't look embarrassed anymore. In fact, it looked as though he and Gwen were having, for the first time since Terry could recall, a serious and almost private conversation.

"Well, what-da-you-know", he thought out loud, as he joined the group.

"You'll be there then?" Karl asked

"Wouldn't miss it for the world Reverend," Burt Walker committed.

"Terry," his mother said as he joined the group,

"Reverend Watts is having a special service tomorrow morning at church. You remember church don't you, son?" I know it's been a long time since you've been, but I'm sure it will come back to you. Will you join us tomorrow morning?"

Terry Habersham hadn't been to, church services in over...a year..two..three...maybe three years. He had gone every Sunday while living at home but had gotten out of the habit while away at college. When he returned home, after graduation, he just hadn't started back up. Church wasn't a mandatory thing in their home. It was just something that you did on Sunday mornings if you were a Habersham. Well, if you were a Habersham and wanted to get up on a Sunday morning and join the rest of the family. It wasn't that he didn't want to go, he'd just gotten out of the habit.

Now in front of all these people, his mother had just given him a dig about not attending. What was he to say?

"Sure, I'll join you. What's going on special tomorrow?" He asked, and the others standing there began to tell him about Bill Junior.

As they talked, Evelyn leaned over to Ted and whispered,

"Have you heard from Bud Johnson? Is he coming?"

Ted Whispered back,

"No, Bud won't be coming this evening."

Bud had pulled the rope hanging from the door and, when he did, reality came tumbling down. With nothing else to do, he had spent the rest of the afternoon and evening up in his attic, sorting and rummaging through memories. The experience brought clarity and focus. The focus he had lacked for the past few years.

And now here he sat at the head table of yet another major fund raising event. They had cheered his arrival and applauded loudly and long after his introduction. Question was, what would they do after his speech was over? What would he do? As he stood behind the podium, lights glaring in his eyes, Bud Johnson, Senator, began his speech.

"Thank you, Chairman Banks, for that kind and generous introduction," Bud said as he turned from the podium to nod at the man who had just introduced him.

"It's a pleasure to be with you this evening and to see so many familiar faces," he added as he turned back and surveyed the large audience.

"I want you to journey along with me tonight. It's not a journey to the State Senate, or to Capital Hill, nor to the White House. It's a journey to your house, to where you live...to your place.

I want you to walk with me into your house, in through the front door. Up the stairs and to that rope hanging down from the attic door, and I want you to pull on that rope...with me tonight.

Tonight, lets pull the rope, in the attic of our minds, and the flimsy wooden attic stairs will lower, and unfold. They rest on the floor we are standing on, secure and strong enough to support us, we tell ourselves. Climbing a few steps we must clear the cobweb's accumulation, for all that has passed here for months even perhaps years are bugs and flies. Only the spider has feasted in the attic these past fleeing years. Only they have seen "Fidelity," lying over in the corner gathering dust.

Cleared away by the sweep of our hand, cobwebs and their content fall aside as we step from the light of the hallway into the darkness of the attic. "What has been happening up here all these years?" we ask ourselves, as our hands grope in the dark for the string dangling from that signal light bulb. We are eager to find the string, eager to eliminate the darkness, eager to shed some light on all that is in the attic, eager to be able to see...for it is true...we are, even as adults...afraid of the dark. We live in it, but we're afraid of it.

Finding the string we quickly pull, and light floods the darkness of our minds. Quickly but cautiously our eyes scan the dusty attic. We are alone. It is safe to be here. We take one step forward and our eyes look down at the creaky floor beneath our feet and lying there is an old Bible given to us years earlier, the one we promised to read from cover to cover. But then we remember that newer Bible downstairs and try to excuse ourselves for not reading this one in the attic by thinking,

"It's the one downstairs I'm going to read from cover to cover." Knowing, as we think the excuse, we will probably never read any Bible from cover to cover.

"Life is too short," we think. "And it's such a big book to read. It's around all the time. Give me a new best-seller, about eight hundred pages long, and I'll read it."

Hastily thumbing through the pages of the once prized…now discarded Bible, we are stopped by an envelope inserted between its pages. Opening the yellowed envelope we find our signed Baptismal Certificate. The one given to us years earlier when we knelt to receive Christ's free gift. Standing there in the attic we read its message again: Presented to us on that day, by that minister, by that Church, by Jesus Christ, by God. In our own handwriting we see and remember writing, 'God, I give you my all.'

Closing and laying the old attic Bible aside to accumulate even more dust, its pages eaten along the edges by rodents-at least they have tasted of it's contents and found themselves filled these past few years- we step cautiously on the creaky boards of the attic floor towards the dustiest corner. There our eyes fall again along the way on another item of remembrance. It's the picture album of our wedding day. Picking it up and wiping off its cover we open the album to be shocked once again at the many pictures of the two youthful participants. Love had been so real back then. It filled every waking moment. It guided our dreams. We longed to be with one another and managed our lives in order to be. When we were a part, it was as though half of us was missing and when together we were as one. He looked so handsome, she so beautiful, in those pictures taken on that special day. The piece of cake he shoved into her mouth, the one with her and Dad walking down the isle. But years had cooled their burning love. Years had turned down the flame.

Years had adjusted their love from that of a steaming heat, to that of a lukewarm and often even chilling flow.

There inside the picture album of their wedding day, was the secret letter found just a few weeks earlier. The other partner had found it. Brought it up into the attic. Placed it there. It was a letter written to the other partner in these pictures…a letter, which revealed unfaithfulness. With tears welling up in the eyes, the album is quickly closed, sealing the letter again inside. Laying the dusty album aside, we say to ourselves, 'After all, I'm up here looking for "Fidelity."' Where is it, where is it?

Stepping again along the dusty attic floor we arrive and are almost afraid to reach down and put our hands into the corner where we hope to find 'Fidelity.' But, we have come this far and so with great caution and hesitancy, we reach slowly towards the pile of dusty items there in the corner and lift from the rubble, 'Commitment.'

We vaguely remember 'Commitment.' Commitment is what we used to do. Commitment is what we did on our wedding day. We made a commitment to our partners. We made a commitment to be there for them if one became ill. We made a commitment to be there in good times and in bad times. We made a commitment to support one another…to encourage one another…to pray for one another…to love one another. We committed our selves to one another. Even after we had committed our lives to that other partner, and it had not worked, we committed our lives again to the new partner even more determined in our commitment. We remember 'Commitment.' What is it doing up here in this dusty old attic we ask ourselves, while hastily rubbing off as much of the dust as we can and carrying it to the top of the attic stairs determined to carrying it back down with us when we go. Downstairs, we tell ourselves, we will clean up our commitment and place it in the center of our home.

Again in the dustiest corner of the attic we reach down and pull up from the pile 'Loyalty.' Who put 'Loyalty' up here? I did not tell anyone to bring it to this filthy place. Loyalty was once part of our daily lives.

We were loyal to our friends. We were loyal to our parents. We were loyal to our partner in marriage. We were loyal to our business associates. We were loyal to our values, our principals, our personal platforms, and our commitments. We were loyal to our Church. We were loyal to Jesus Christ. Who brought 'Loyalty' up here? We want to know! And so 'Loyalty' joins, 'Commitment' at the top of the attic steps. It will be taken down, cleaned up and placed in a prominent place along with, 'Commitment,' when we descend the stairs shortly.

Walking to the dusty corner again we reach down and pull up one of the two remaining items: 'Integrity.' Oh, how we thought we had lost our 'Integrity'! That which sets us apart from the crowd. That which assures us of our uniqueness. That which founded our self esteem. That which lifted us, surrounded us, assured us...our 'Integrity'!

Proudly hold it up and wipe off the dust and place it at the top of the steps with 'Commitment' and 'Loyalty'. Smiling within and out, for we found our Integrity. Assured of the success of our search, we walk sure-footed upon the creaky, dusty attic boards back over to the dustiest corner and pick up the last item laying there: 'Fidelity!' We pull from our bag a clean rag and wipe 'Fidelity'...but it will not come clean. Another rag from our bag, we try again, but it will not wipe clean. None of the dust will come off. NONE!

We walk to the top of the stairs and grab 'Commitment', 'Loyalty', 'Integrity' and descend the stairs so rapidly that we almost miss a few runs of the latter and fall and break our neck, but at last we make it to the bottom safe with contents still in hand.

We run to the sink and turn on the faucet. Filling the sink, we reach for the strongest detergent, plunging 'Fidelity' into the steam. We wipe, then scrub and scrub and scrub....but it will not come clean! Try and try and try again it is not until we are totally exhausted that we cease trying to clean up 'Fidelity' and slump, totally exhausted, almost out of breath, on the floor.

'Fidelity,' means to be faithful. To have great devotion. To have allegiance. To adore. To be consecrated, set a part...aside, reserved.

'Infidelity' means to be unfaithful. To have no consistency between what one says, one believes, and the actions in one's daily life.

They say one thing and do the other.

They say they love everyone, but treat others with contempt.

They gather in numbers to exert power, not to lift in prayer, but to bring down and destroy.

They talk the talk, but don't walk the walk.

They are infidels.

They are the worst of the worst.

Jesus Christ was crucified, by a radical religious right-wing faction of his faith. Put the spikes and hammers away!"

And Bud Johnson turned away from the podium, walked back over and took his seat.

...and silence reigned throughout the great hall.

Chapter twelve
RISING TO THE OCCASION

Burt Walker had started his nightly tour of places to sleep at about midnight. He long ago had given up the dream of going to bed and winding up there in the morning. His hope was to sleep in one of his designated locations, within the house, one or two hours at a time, before his inner alarm jerked him awake. By four in the morning he had already hit two locations and was sitting back up in he and Nancy's bedroom, in his favorite rocking chair by the front window, half reading, when he heard the car pull into the driveway.

Burt reached his finger over and separated the sheers in the window. He didn't recognize the car but did recognize Jerrey as he peeled himself out of the car and walked sleepily in through the front door of their house. Burt continued to watch as the unidentified car pulled slowly out of his driveway and up the street, away from the house.

He heard Jerrey quietly climbing the stairs and so Burt reached over and turned off the light he was using. After all Jerrey was twenty years old now and his Dad didn't want Jerrey to think he was still keeping tabs on him. As Jerrey walked down the hall closer to the bedrooms, Burt listened as he sat in the dark quietness. Just before Jerrey entered his own bedroom he said,

"Night, Dad".

"Night, Jerrey," his Dad responded, and smiled to himself.

As Burt sat there in the dark, his mind thought back over the years with Jerrey. He had been a good kid with average grades in school. Hadn't gotten into any trouble to speak of, and now that he was a young man he was kind of fun to have around. Not that he wasn't fun before, it was just different. It

149

was like having both a son and a young friend in the house. A buddy. Burt knew it wouldn't last much longer. Jerrey had become even closer friends with Terry Habersham, and Terry was motivated. Eventually that would rub off onto Jerrey, Burt thought. Youth and motivation had a habit of growing together.

Sitting in his rocker beside the front window, Burt's mind reflected back on his youth. Days gone by that could not be recaptured, days of growing up in that small town in Kansas. That was probably the reason he finally settled down here in this small town. Days of climbing the corporate latter; of giving his all. Days of devotion to a company whose motto was, "We care about you." And that had been the case with Burt and his company, for a while anyway. They had cared about Burt and Nancy. Burt had been the top salesman for the entire North American operation. He had been promoted to the International Headquarters in Montreal, Canada, and was considered one of the fast-track boys. During one of his many flights to a major branch, he had met Nancy. She had been one of the stewardesses on his plane and, though it was a definite taboo for passenger and stewardess to mix, they had worked it out. Several dates, and six months later they both knew it was real. His company had paid all her expenses to move her to Montreal. His company had been wonderful to both of them. Had been. But when Nancy became pregnant with their first child and he suggested cutting back on his traveling, the company took him off the fast track and put him on the slower one. Eventually, because he always put his family first, Burt was downsized out of the company. Years later now, sitting there in the early morning hours, he reconfirmed his earlier decision. Family came first, regardless.

It hadn't always been that way with Burt. There was a time when family came second and the career, such as it was, came first. He could remember when just a good career opportunity was all that he wanted. Just to find a company that would give him a chance to prove his worth. But in the middle of his search, his entire battalion had been activated and sent to Vietnam. In fact, he knew it was while he was serving in the Central Highlands of Vietnam that the root core to his values, his guiding principals; his attitude about life was being reshaped.

In Vietnam, Burt had seen babies just old enough to crawl living in cardboard refrigerator carton lean-twos, fighting with the older boys and girls for something to eat. He witnesses children and women fighting over American soldier's garbage, for that was how they survived. Soldiers behaving like hooligans, and victims, everywhere. There were some things Burt had never spoken of, not even now. They were unspeakable memories. Some he had witnessed, others he had committed in the name of justifiable war. Following orders could leave lasting memories, families torn apart and shattered. With out question, it was while he was in Vietnam that his attitude about life and the family had started to change. So that when Burt started his own family the career, not the family, was put on the back burner. And he had been blessed because of that change in attitude. Nancy and the children had been a gift to him, he believed, a precious gift to cherish.

Sitting there in his rocker, Burt confirmed to himself...family first...family first.

Sunday

At twilight, that special time between night and day, before the sunrise, the man in the dark brown overcoat with a red scarf around his neck moved silently and reverently into the Sanctuary of the small church. He walked down the center aisle of that consecrated place, and approached the prayer rail. Once there, he looked down and knew that many a saint had knelt where he was about to. Many a fervent prayer had been offered up, for delivery before the throne.

It was his custom to rise before the sun and offer his prayers, and today would be no exception. As he bent his knees to kneel on the cushion and reached out his hands to grasp the polished mahogany rail, a sense of eternal presence and power flooded his spirit. Human ears would not hear his words, offered in prayer, but all heaven would hear them and move to fulfill His will.

He prayed for the saints and those who would be. He prayed for grace and mercy. He prayed for those who would be meeting in this Sanctuary, on this day...and he left, even more quietly and reverently then he had entered.

Grandma Habersham was in pain. She had taken only half the medicine Betsy had prescribed for her because when she took the full dosage, she felt woozy. When various members of the family had asked her recently,

"Grandma have you taken your medicine"?

she would always answer,

"Yes I have." She just never said how much of it she had taken.

She had decided that she'd rather be in a little pain, and have total control of all her faculties, then walk around half stoopered all the time. But that decision was becoming more difficult to keep. The pain was getting worse and, this morning, it was pretty bad.

Not able to sleep, Grandma snuck down the stairs, out of the back door of her home and walked out into the backfield toward the tree line several hundred yards away. Mist was rising slowly from the noisy frog pond and birds were starting their early morning songs. Grandma wanted to pray, had to pray, but the words would not come at first. She knew the end was near for her, Betsy had told her days ago. It had come as a shock to Betsy but not to her grandmother. It had been so hard for Betsy to tell her. "The dear child" she thought.

Now, the pain was getting worse. How long could she hold out before taking more of that medicine? As she looked around at the beauty of the place in which she was standing, words came back to her and with tears filling her eyes, she said;

"Oh, dear God, you have been so good to us...so good to me. The pain is getting worse...and I'm getting so tired.... God..."

Ted watched his mother, from he and Evelyn's bedroom balcony on the back of the house. He had never seen his mother in her bathrobe standing in the middle of the field before. It was obvious to him and everyone in the family that she wasn't taking her medicine. Betsy had told them the medicine would make her woozy. But his mother wasn't woozy at all. That meant only one thing, but that was okay with Ted. He knew her pretty well by now. Woozy she wouldn't want. Not his Mom. Whatever the consequences were, she'd suffer with them rather then be woozy and not in total control.

Now there she stood in the field praying, it seemed. How many times, when he was a little body, had she prayed with him? What a lasting impression that had left with him. *She hadn't been a perfect mom, but she had tried and that said something didn't it?* Ted thought as he stood there watching her.

"What's she doing?" Evelyn asked, as she slipped up behind Ted and put her arms around him.

"Praying I guess," Ted answered..."Praying."

On the other side of town, Bill Junior sat in Hnob Good Park, watching the sunrise over the pines. To Bill Junior this was a special time in each day...The beginning...again.

He knew that h e wasn't like the others. He wasn't as smart like they were. Sometimes Bill Junior wished he wasn't as smart as he was, then he wouldn't know that he could have been smarter and wasn't. It seemed to him like he was in between. Between being as smart as all the others, and being even not as smart as he was. But, while in some ways he wasn't as smart as all the others, in some ways he thought he was smarter. Like now, watching the sun come up again. Most all the others could care less about the sun rising. But to Bill Junior it was a special time, because he knew it was another whole new beginning. Yesterday was gone and no one, not even the smartest ones could get it back. So all the things done wrong yesterday were gone with yesterday. That made today, a brand new start. He knew even most of the smartest people didn't know that, because they always talked about yesterday and the things they had done wrong, like they were suppose to carry all the yesterdays around with them and bring them into today.

But not Bill Junior. No buddy! He knew that this was a whole new day.

A whole new day. And for Bill Junior, this was going to be a very special day. Today, he was going to be baptized into the church. It meant a lot to him. Being baptized into the church meant he and God would be even closer then they were now. And Bill Junior thought that would really be cool. He also knew it meant a lot to other people. People like his folks. They had been on the phone with him for weeks now, calling all their relatives and friends, telling them about today and Bill Junior's Baptism, inviting them to church. Some said they would be there, he didn't know how many. But he hoped some would come.

As the sun rose higher, Bill Junior knew he needed to get back home so he prayed his morning prayer. He had made it up himself.

"Dear God, Hi! It's me Bill Junior, one of your children. Thanks for this day. Thanks for Mom and Dad and Rev. Karl. If you need some help doing something today, just let me know. You have a good day, too. Amen"

In the still of the morning, Jill and Tom lay in their new bed together staring at the ceiling. Each was trying not to disturb the other, but neither had slept much during the night. Their thoughts, though separate, were joined together and focused on the same set of question. "What did the future hold?" "How had they come to meet this man and woman, so generous?" "What would today be like for them but, most importantly, for their kids?"

When the telephone rang, they both jumped completely out of bed. Neither knew there was a phone in this place. The shock of its ringing froze them in place for a few seconds. Then Tom started toward the noise and picked up the receiver.

"Hello," he said, tentatively.

"Tom? Bill Senior. Just called to remind you all about breakfast this morning."

"Breakfast?" Tom questioned.

"Yes, at Shelley's. You met her last night."

"Oh, yes, I forgot."

"We'll be leaving in about forty-five minutes. That enough time for you all?" Bill Senior asked.

"Sure. We'll be ready," Tom said, and the phone went dead.

"Breakfast," Jill said, "I forgot," and she ran into the kids room as Tom stood there looking at the phone.

Karl had been awake for five minutes when his alarm, sitting on the nightstand beside their bed, stated making it's usual racket. He really didn't now why he set the thing. He was always awake before it started ringing. Habit, he guessed, or maybe it was the fear of not waking on time. He didn't know. But it had been months, at least, since the alarm had beaten him. He reached over and turned the commotion off quickly before it woke Alice. *Before it woke Alice...and the baby,* he thought, smiling from ear to ear, at the thought. He reached over and kissed her on the cheek and slid out of bed. It was six o'clock.

By seven, he was in his car driving the short distance between their home and the church. He enjoyed this drive on Sunday mornings. It was so quiet this time of day during the week and, on Sundays, even quieter. During the week, on occasion, he would see a jogger or two, but not this morning. *They must sleep in on Sundays.* He thought, as he drove into the Church's parking lot.

As Karl drove to his designated space located at the back of the building, he noticed that Martin Outer, the church's custodian had beaten him again. Karl knew it was a game Martin played, beating the minister to church on Sunday mornings. He knew Martin would say, "Afternoon Reverend," as soon as he saw him. Karl kept promising himself that one Sunday he was going to get to the church at about three in the morning, that should do it. But then again, he wasn't sure Martin just didn't stay here on Saturday nights just to beat him.

As he walked toward the all glass back door of the church building, Karl saw Martin standing inside and knew it was coming;

"Afternoon Reverend," Martin said, as he unlocked and opened the back door.

"Afternoon, Martin. Did you sleep here last night again?" Karl asked.

"No Reverend, didn't...Just got up on time," Martin added with delight.

"Coffee's already done in the kitchen." Martin added

"Who made it?" Karl asked, as he walked down the hall

"Well, I did, of course," Martin answered.

"Lord help us. Will a spoon stand up in it by itself?" Karl asked.

"Well you see fore yourself Reverend," Martin said.

156

"I'll be down later, my friend," Karl said as he continued down the hall.

It was the same conversation the two carried on each Sunday morning upon Karl's arrival and both men enjoyed the bantering and friendship immensely. It was seven twenty.

Like most days during the week, Karl's first act on Sunday mornings was to walk into his office and turn on the lights. His second act was to walk into the Sanctuary and have a period of time by himself with God. This morning, Karl moved quietly into the Sanctuary of the small church he had been given charge of. He moved quietly, silently and reverently down the central aisle of that consecrated space and approached the prayer rail. As he bent his knees toward the cushion, he reached out and grasped the wooden prayer rail.

Today was going to be an important day in the life of his congregation. A Baptism, a sacrament, a sacred event, but this day had also been designated as Communion, Holy Eucharist Sunday, also a sacrament, a sacred event.

The possibility of several new people in worship was great due to the Baptism, not to mention the Smith family and their anxiety. Surely, Christ would be present with them not only because the saints would be here to worship, but because of the two sacraments.

Karl had worked on his short sermon for days now, so little time to say so much. Some of those in worship today may not be back. They may only be here today because of Bill Junior and his family's efforts. Some may drop in just to try the worship experience. Some, simply out of curiosity, may come by. Karl never knew how many would show up and where they came from once here. Everyone would be asked to register their atendance, some would but a few wouldn't. He was always afraid it was the ones who failed to register that needed help the most…so little time to say so much.

He prayed that his sermon, or more like a short Homily as they called it, would be what they needed to hear, that the words of his mouth and the inspiration of his heart would be what they needed to hear. He prayed that Christ would be present with them and in the Communion, Holy Eucharist elements themselves. He prayed that the congregation would accept the Smiths...and then he started naming each member and family in the congregation as he lifted each of them up in prayer. His prayer would come to its conclusion only after he had lifted each of them and all of them up in prayer.

Ashley was still lying in bed, half asleep, when she smelled the sweet aroma of cinnamon rolls and knew Shelley was downstairs preparing breakfast. The restaurant wasn't open on Sundays but Shelley promised, last night at the party, to fix her famous Cinnamon rolls for Bill Junior and his family this morning.

Ashley moved very quietly as she pulled on a pair of blue jeans, slipped on a pair of sandals, threw on a top and headed downstairs. Shelley was just pulling a sheet pan of cinnamon rolls out of the oven as Ashley entered the restaurant. "How can I help?" Ashley asked, as she approached the oven. "Well, how about handing me that sheet pan?" Shelley asked. "Have a good time last night?" Shelley inquired.

"Yes we did. It was really good for Mom to get out and Sammy had fun with the other kids."

Shelley knew by Ashley's answer that the party would have been better in Ashley's mind if there had been some teenagers there.

"Yeah, know exactly what you mean." Shelley said. "Think we all could eat up in your apartment this morning." she asked.

"Of course Shelley. I'll go up and set up the kitchen table," Ashley said, as she headed for the stairs.

The problem was, Shelley didn't know any teenagers.

"All the teenagers are in school," she thought.

Well, there you have it. When Katherine took the two kids over to register them in school, then Ashley would meet some teenagers.

Shelley was in the middle of her thoughts and just taking another sheet pan out of the oven when she heard a knock at the side door. She was just about ready to yell for Ashley when the teenager said,

"I've got it."

Shelley heard Ashley unlock the side door and the unmistakable voices of Bill Junior and his mother as they entered the building. She knew his father and that other couple- what were their names? Oh yes, Smith. Yes they,- would be back there too. She had invited them all.

"Well, why not?" she thought. "I love this business and the people who come here on a regular basis. If I would feel right being open on Sundays, I'd be open seven days a week," she told herself. They loved Shelley's cooking and she needed them.

Few people knew Shelley's story. She thought,

"Everybody has a story. Who would want to listen to mine?" and so only a few had heard her story, only those who had to. Only the Sheriff and Police Chief. They needed to know. They had to know. But in all the time she had been here, she couldn't remember telling her story to anyone else. Maybe someday, some one would be interested in her story. Someone she could trust, maybe someday.

"Ash,"...she called.

Terry was stepping out of the shower when he remembered promising to attend worship services today. Usually on Sunday mornings he went into the office for a couple hours. All the younger members of the small law firm went in on Sunday mornings. It was the older members of the firm who went to church.

It wasn't that he accomplished that much by going in on Sunday mornings, it was just what the younger attorneys did. It was, 'cool', the thing to do, 'politically correct', 'a power move', to go in on Sunday mornings. In fact, some of the younger attorneys thought it 'corny', 'hooky' and a 'cop out', to attend worship services on Sunday mornings. It was what 'weak' people did. Well, no doubt they would have something to say about his going to church today. But a promise was a promise.

The smell of breakfast filled Grandpa's house as he walked down the stairs and long hall into the kitchen. His father and mother were sitting at the kitchen table with his grand mother when he entered.

"Morning, son," his father said.

"Morning." Terry replied.

"Did you have a good sleep last night," his mother asked.

"Slept like a log, as a mater of fact." Terry answered.

"Morning grandma." Terry said, as he looked over her head at his parents. They both sipped on their coffee cups and looked at him with their eyes. Everyone knew what no one would say. Everyone. "Good morning, Terry," his grand mother said.

"Morning Terry." Mary said as she brought him a plate heaped high with eggs, hash browns, grits, bacon and toast, her Southern breakfast, as she called it.

"Good morning Mary, and thanks," he said.

"You're welcome," she said. Coffee?"

"Please," he answered.

"Are you riding with us to church this morning Terry or are you going to drive yourself?" his mother asked.

Cute, he thought. It was his mother's way of asking him if he was going with them to worship or into the office. When he looked up from his plate to answer his mother, she was looking down at her plate and so he looked at his father out of the corner of his eye, winked and said,

"church?"

His humor, which his mother did not catch, was not lost on his grand mother who looked over at him and smiled before she joined the others waiting for Evelyn's response.

His mother took the hook. "Don't you remember, last evening on the Verandah, promising Rev. Watts that you'd be in worship this morning? It's a very special day and--." Evelyn stopped in mid sentence when she realized what was going on. She had to think fast and get back at her son for his--."Don't forget to do something with your hair before you go," she said, and everyone caught the humor of the moment.

While Terry had always, 'pulled his mother's leg,' when given a chance, even as a little boy, she had always kidded him about his hair. Terry's hair was very important to him. He went to the stylist at least twice a month and sometimes every week. Every hair had to be in place, as it was this morning.

"Where are Betsy and Gwen?" Terry asked.

"Betsy went into the hospital early. Said she'd be in church today though. Gwen, I think is still upstairs in bed," Mary answered.

"I'd better go up and get her moving," Evelyn said, as she stood, took her plate over to the sink, and walked out of the kitchen.

Upstairs in her daughter's room, Evelyn pulled the dark curtains back away from the windows and opened the blinds. Gwen's room was on the east side of the house, which allowed the full sun to shine in through the windows and brighten the room as though floodlights had just been turned on. Gwen's head, which had been halfway buried under the covers, vanished immediately upon the sun's intrusion.

"Gwen, honey, your store's on fire and someone stole all your Lilac. You'd better get up and go see about it," her mother said, as she tugged at the covers.

"What time is it?" Gwen asked from under the covers.

"It's time to get up for church"

"church?" Gwen asked.

"Yes, church. Gwen, where's your car honey? Why are you driving a rental car?" "It's a long story mom. Later," Gwen said.

"Okay, later it is. But come on now," Evenly said as she left Gwen's room knowing her daughter would be up and ready on time.

"Jerrey?" his Dad said, as he shoved and pulled the bundle of blankets back and forth. "Jerrey, get up. There's this beautiful blonde waiting for you downstairs. Says she wants to see you right away."

"You talk to her Dad," Jerrey answered, his head buried under the covers and his face in his pillow. After all, he had heard this one before. It was one of several lines his Dad had used over the years to get him up in the mornings.

"Gwen Habersham phoned," his Dad said next.

"What?" Jerrey said, as the covers moved off of him and he sat upright in the middle of his bed.

"Thought that might work," his dad said, as he walked out of his son's room. "Come to breakfast," Burt added, as he continued down the hall.

"Cute," Jerrey said, disgustingly. "Real cute."

Around town, similar events were taking place in the homes of numerous families as they rose to the occasion. It was Sunday morning and more and more families were setting this time aside for Worship.

Chapter Thirteen
THE MAIN EVENT

After the breakfast dishes had been put into the dishwasher and the kitchen straightened up, Mary straightened herself up and left the big house for church. Her church.

She hadn't missed a Sunday for years now. Even on those Sundays when she really didn't feel like going, she went anyway and after worship, she always felt better. Her church was on the other side of town away from any of the other churches in town. Her church was a "Black" church, as many of the folks around town called it. Its official name was the First African Methodist Episcopal Church, somewhat part of the United Methodist Church but then again, not really.

The building had been built decades ago when segregation or separation was not only accepted but also mandated. Today, that was not the case. The congregation had thought about moving up with the other churches and rebuilding several times, but each time had decided to stay put. After all, to replace or even move the beautiful stain glass windows would be very costly and there was no way the congregation could afford to build the same quality of building. So they stayed where they were, not because they had to any more, but because they chose to. Nevertheless, Sunday morning was still the most segregated morning in Methodism. While there were African American congregations within the United Methodist system, they were few and far between.

Mary never thought that much about the whole thing. She had grown up going to her church, meeting her mother and father there each Sunday while they were still alive, and while the Habershams had invited her to their church more then once, she had always begged off and continued going to

163

her church over the years. She knew everyone there and they all knew her. It was like a homecoming each Sunday at her church and Mary needed the home coming more often then not. *Especially this Sunday* Mary thought.

Everyone in the Habersham family, which included her, knew that Mrs. Habersham, Grandma, would be leaving shortly. And no one would feel the loss any more than Mary. Mary had been there with Mr. and Mrs. Habershams before Teddy, before Evelyn. Before grandchildren or anyone else. Through the years they had grown so close; "like sisters as such," Mary thought as she drove to her church.

She had considered going with the rest of the family over to Reverend Watt's church today, but grandma had told Mary that while she was invited and welcome, to do what ever she wanted to do. If she wanted to go to Reverend Watt's church that would be fine but if she wanted to go to her own church, well that would be all right too. The family would understand and she was sure Reverend Watts would too.

"You do what you want to do, Mary," was what Grandma had said. And so, Mary had decided to go on to her own church this morning. But sitting in the parking lot of her church, she began to wonder if her decision was the right one.

Betsy had planed on going directly from the hospital to the church service, but as happened all too often as far as she was concerned, she hadn't planned well enough. She had forgotten her heels and didn't favor the idea of wearing the black dress she had thrown into her car into church with white hospital oxfords on. It would take about twenty-five minutes to run home, pick up her black heels and get to church on time. Simply leaving the hospital a half hour earlier would easily solve the problem, or so she thought.

Karl had joined the Men's Club in the fellowship hall for their monthly breakfast meeting and as usual ate much more then he had planned. One of the men had given a short devotional at the meeting that Karl felt came straight from the heart. It was quite good, as far as Karl was concerned and so he made a special point to tell the speaker so after the meeting.

By the time Karl left the meeting, Martin Outer, the custodian, had unlocked all the doors and turned on all the lights and heat. Scott Thompson, the assistant minister, had arrived and was in his study putting on his robe and stole. Kay Carol, the organist and Myra Rice, the choir director, were practicing. And this month's head usher- *what is his name?* Karl asked himself, frantically. "For goodness sake...what...? Blair Hatfield," he said out loud, pleased at himself for finally remembering the man's name. But Blair thought Karl was greeting him from all the way down the hall and turned to respond.

"Morning Reverend how are you today?" The head usher said, feeling very important that out of all the members of this church Reverend Watts had remembered his name.

"Fine Blair. It's a great day in the making, isn't it?"

"Morning Reverend," came a familiar and happy voice. It was Bill Jr. Though this was his day to be baptized, it was also his scheduled month to serve as one of the greeters, and he had insisted on doing both today.

"Morning Bill Junior. Where are your folks?" Karl asked.

"They're coming. They dropped me off then had to go pick up some more people." He answered.

"Great!" Karl said as he walked on into his study and changed into his robe and stole. The cross he chose to wear this morning had been given to him by one of the members of the congregation. She had picked it up for Karl, during one of her trips to the Holy Land. After checking himself in the mirror, Karl took a half dozen mints out of the glass jar sitting on his file cabinet and placed them under his robe, in the front pocket of his slacks. With everything in order, he hoped, Karl exited his study and headed for the main entrance. He smiled at his thoughts as he walked toward the front of the building. That boxing announcer always said; "This is the main event."

"How wrong," Karl thought.
"This, Sunday Morning worship,
THIS IS, the MAIN EVENT!"

Betsy left the car door open and the motor running, as she
ran up the sidewalk and into the front door of the house. It
would only take a minute to grab her shoes. She was headed
for the stairs, when she heard her father say from the kitchen
hall way;
"Do you think we'd better call Betsy?"
"Why call me?" she thought, "I'm here."
She turned and walked down the hallway toward her father.
When he saw her coming he seemed a little surprised but not
startled.
"What's up"? Betsy asked.
"It's mom," Ted said.
"She says she's not feeling very well. Not well enough to go
to church and you know that must be pretty bad Betsy, for
her to miss church."
"I'll take a look at her," Betsy said.
As she walked into he kitchen, Betsy could tell that her
grand mother was in pain. Probably a lot of pain.
"Grandma, did you take your medicine this morning?"
"Yes, I did," her grand mother answered.
"All of it?" Betsy asked.
"This morning, all of it," her grandma answered.
That could mean only one thing: Things were getting worse
in a hurry. Betsy turned to her dad and said,
"Dad, why don't you give Grandma a big hug, go on to
church, and I'll stay home with her this morning. You and
mom go on to church. Grandma and I'll have church here
this morning."
Ted looked at his mother sitting at the kitchen table and then
at his daughter standing beside her. He knew without a
shadow of doubt what Betsy had just told him, "...give
grandma a big hung...", Ted knew what Betsy was saying, it
might very well be the last hug he would be giving her this
side of Heaven.

Oh, Mom, Ted thought, d*on't leave me.* His mother had not always been the warmest mother, but she loved him, and he knew it. All those years of growing up in his mother's and Mary's arms, came rushing back to Ted as he stood there looking at her, all those years in this house with her. She had always been there for him. Always. Now, he knew, that time was swiftly coming to and end, and he didn't want it to. He turned and looked at Evelyn and saw in her eyes the desire to stay home with her mother-in-law and Betsy this morning...and Grandma saw it, too.

"Now listen you two, I'm not going anywhere. I just don't feel up to going to church this morning, for goodness sake. Let's not put me in the ground yet. You two go on to church and say a prayer for me. Betsy and I will stay home and like she said, have church here this morning. Tell Reverend Karl to drop by tomorrow afternoon and see me if he has time. Now go on with you. For goodness sake. Betsy's a Doctor and all. Go on, Evelyn. Ted..."

And so Ted walked over to his mother, relieved that he had obviously jumped the gun, and gave her a hug. A big hung. She even hugged back, which was not always her custom.

"I love you, Mom," Ted said.

"I love you too Teddy," his mother said as they embraced. Evelyn and grandma hugged each other and then Grandma shooed them out the door. There was no debate, no argument, and no discussion. Betsy and her were going to stay home together this morning and Ted and Evelyn, just like Gwen and Terry who had already left, were going to church.

On the second Sunday after his appointment and arrival as Senior Pastor of the small congregation, Karl asked Scott Thompson, the Assistant Minister to follow him outside. It was a half hour before the Sunday morning worship service. From that Sunday on, both of them were out in front of the church's building waving at all the cars that drove by and those that drove into the parking lot. They had been doing it for over two years now. Neither Karl nor Scott knew how many passer-bys had eventually decided to worship with them, but they both knew some had. Besides, they both had fun standing out in front of the church's building waving and greeting those who had parked in the lot and walked up the sidewalk toward them. The smiles on everyone's faces as they drove by and honked their horns or walked up the sidewalk and greeted the two men was enough to make you want to do it next Sunday, and they had, each Sunday for over two years now.

As one car after the other drove by or pulled into the parking lot, the two men smiled and waved with great excitement, it wasn't a put-on or faked excitement. It was real, for both men shared the same belief...THIS WAS THE MAIN EVENT!

Several families had already entered the building. Some Karl and Scott knew, some they didn't, when Gwen Habersham walked up the sidewalk toward them. Now Ron Thompson was still a single man with an eye for some of God's greatest creations. "You know, Karl," Ron said just loud enough for the both of them to hear,

"Every time I see her, I want to sing the Doxology." Both men smiled a little broader as Gwen came within earshot.

"Good morning Miss Habersham," Scott said formally as he extended his hand.

"Morning Mr. Thompson," Gwen replied in the same formal manner.

When she reached out her hand to Karl, she asked,

"What's with him this morning?" nodding toward Scott.

"Oh, Gwen, he's been fantasizing about finding a beautiful woman again...then you started up the walk," Karl said as he winked at her.

She smiled and knew it was the truth as she continued into the church's building. Scott Thompson had been giving her the eye for the last six months now, but he hadn't found the courage to ask her out...shame..."Wimp!"

Several other families drove up and walked into the building before the Walkers arrived. Karl noticed that Burt and his wife,- *What was her name?* arrived in their car and Jerrey in his "Beautiful." Well today, not-so-beautiful car. Right behind them, Shelley, from the restaurant with the same name, and some others with her drove up and parked. Ted and Evelyn Habersham were mixed in with the next group that arrived and Bud Johnson walked in just behind Terry Habersham. Bill Senior looked like the pied piper as he lead them. Karl and Ron didn't know how many people, families into the building. Both thought they might want to baptize Bill Junior again next week and the week after, if doing so would bring this many people out to worship each week.

People were still coming up the sidewalk when Karl said, "It's eleven o'clock, Scott," and both men turned and entered the building through the main two glass doors. They both knew that people would be coming up the sidewalk, into the building and Sanctuary through the first fifteen minutes of worship. But it was time...It was time.

Karl couldn't help it. His excitement level increased to the bursting point.

"THIS WAS THE MAIN EVENT!", he thought, as he stood just outside the Sanctuary. People were still filing into the Sanctuary greeting him, and he them.

The choir sometimes processed in, but this morning Karl had asked if they could already be in place and singing fifteen minutes before the service was to begin. They had been, and the mood of the congregation was warm and filled to the brim with anticipation. Karl had picked out some hymns and other music he wanted the choir to sing during this period of time, and Myra had agreed whole-heartedly, which was not always the case. Not new hymns, but some of the old ones he felt most of the worshipers would know. Karl realized that the Sanctuary would be filled today with many who had not been in worship in a long time, perhaps for years, and he wanted to connect with them if possible.

The choir had already sung portions of "Amazing Grace, how sweet the sound." "This is my Father's world." "Jesus means all the world to me." "The world is one foundation." "Love lifted me." and Karl had thrown in "Jesus Christ is risen today", though Easter was a long way off. You could feel it in the air, or better said, "you could feel Him in the air." And Karl was ready to sing.

At precisely eleven o'clock,-"not a minute before nor a minute after," Karl had said, "God is always, right on time."-the choir, which had been singing while sitting in their chairs, rose in unison and invited the congregation to do the same. At the precise moment Kay broke into the first stanza of Charles Wesley's, "Oh for a thousand tongues to sing." and it sounded like ten thousand tongues were singing. Kay had put the pedal to the metal on the organ, the choir was well warmed up and the congregation was ready to join in. Down the center aisle walked two junior high kids carrying candle torches and, following them, Jeremy Slatter, a six foot one-inch teenager dressed in a white robe holding out in front of himself and up high the cross, atop a polished wood and brass pole. Half- way down the aisle, Kay changed pitch, and stomped the organ with several chords as she and the choir broke into "Lift high the cross" And the congregation followed without missing a beat.

Karl was ecstatic.

"THIS IS THE MAIN EVENT!" he wanted to shout, but knew he couldn't or shouldn't. By the time the short precession passed by the prayer rail, where he had knelt earlier that morning in silence, Karl's eyes were over flowing with tears of emotion. As he bowed before the Altar, on which stood a polished and immaculate cross, he knew only by the grace of God was he able to lead this congregation this morning. Rocked with emotion but firm in his appearance, ready to jump out of his skin with excitement but poised and dignified, Karl Watts, pastor of this growing congregation, was ready. Ready to worship God. As the last verse started up, he walked over and behind the Altar, faced the congregation, lifted up his arms while the congregation was still in song, and as the last note sprang forth from their mouths Karl said;

"THE GRACE OF THE LORD JESUS CHRIST BE WITH YOU!" And the congregation sprang back with; "AND ALSO WITH YOU!"

"THE RISEN CHRIST IS WITH US!" Karl said next, as he raised his arms even higher in a gesture of ultimate welcome. "PRAISE BE TO GOD," the congregation responded.

At that precise moment Kay put the pedal to the metal, Myra signaled the choir and they both broke into "We've a story to tell to the nations." The congregation sat down, ready to listen. Those who had been to worship before knew and those who hadn't would soon learn this was the ACT OF PRAISE!

Karl knew from experience that Myra, the choir, and Kay with the organ had practiced this number and whatever else they had planned several times. He never asked. He didn't want to know. He wanted to experience with the congregation this moment of PRAISE! The choir never varied from the main hymn but the music continued to build. Layer upon layer of quartets within the choir sung the same words but at different intervals and Kay at the organ must have pulled out all the stops. The organ sounded like a fifty piece orchestra about ready to jump out of their tuxedoes.

When they were through with the number, the congregation poised on the edge of their pews, sprang to their feet in a thunderous applause. Shouts of "Amen!" could be heard all through the congregation and hands raised in praise sparkled in the Sanctuary's lights. As he stood there applauding with the rest of the congregation, Karl thought, *Now that's how you do an "ACT OF PRAISE!*

He also knew that half the congregations within his own denomination would be having heart attacks about now. Standing and applauding, lifting one's hands in worship and shouting "Amen" just wasn't done anymore. It wasn't dignified. It was too emotional. People and congregations that did such things were considered, 'Charismeniacts', 'Crazy-meneacts' and 'Emotionalizers'. These people, Karl knew, were also the ones who would go to sporting events and yell, scream, and act like lunatics during the week or on Saturday night; but come Sunday morning, they insisted on sitting with their arms, minds and spirits folded in front of them.

Karl hadn't started this movement within his congregation, nor had he tried to stop it. It happened. And since Karl didn't believe anything happened by accident, he felt it must be the work of the Holy Spirit...and Karl wasn't going to get between the Holy Spirit and this congregation. If anything, he was going to open himself up and receive.

In the midst of the applause, Scott Thompson walked to the lectern, the other and smaller pulpit sitting on the front platform, and waited for the applause to stop. After the congregation had been seated once again he announced, "The first lesson for today is found in the Second Chapter of..." and gave the total scripture reference. As Scott read the scripture and the congregation listened, Karl looked out over the gathering. It was even larger than last Easter...than last Christmas, the two Sunday's out of the year when everyone wants to attend worship services and be Christians. *What a moment in time,* Karl thought, "This is truly a day which the Lord has made."

Betsy had helped her grand mother with the few dishes and then they had both walked to the Verandah. There they sat beside each other, in high back rocking chairs, enjoying the view and cool late morning breeze.

"It is beautiful out here," Grandma said.

"Yes it is, Grandma," Betsy replied.

"Did we bring a cup of coffee up here for..."

"We would normally do that in the afternoon, wouldn't we Grandma?"

"Yes, of course, your right. I just thought..."

"What did you think?"

"I just thought it might be...well...well..."

As her grand mother thought through the words she was going to use, Betsy caught a movement over by the doorway leading onto the Veranda. It was Mary. She had returned very early from her Sunday morning worship service, if she had gone at all, Betsy thought. But Betsy understood why.

These two women had drawn closer to one another over the years. Closer then most of the family probably knew.

"I just thought it might be right...Your Grandpas been on my mind lately," grandma said. *Right,* Betsy thought. *Right was the word Grandma had been searching for in her mind. Right...the Right thing to do. Well, maybe it was the right thing to do.*

As Betsy pondered the word, Mary stepped onto the Verandah and walked non-shulaunt over to the serving table.

"We might need to set this table up now," Mary said, as she fiddled with the tablecloth.

"How was church?" Grandma asked.

"Oh, church is always fine Grandma. You know that. I'll get the drinks," Mary said as she walked through the door, back into the house, and disappeared. Betsy knew Mary would bring a mixture of glasses and refreshing drinks; but above all, she would bring a fresh cup of coffee.

At the conclusion of Karl's Homily, he walked to the center of the platform and said,

"Today we are blessed with the celebration of the two sacraments, two sacred events, of the church, The sacrament of Holy Communion, the Holy Eucharist, and the sacrament of Baptism. Today we baptize into the Church of Jesus Christ a young man I have grown to love. Many of you have grown to love him, too. Since he started attending this place of worship, his involvement in the Church's activities has escalated tremendously. He is truly an asset to this congregation. We all bring our various talents and share them...Bill Bright Junior has brought his...and he has shared himself.

This worshipping community is a better place today, because of him and his example. Bill Bright junior, will you present yourself to God and this congregation by coming and standing in front of the prayer rail?"

Before Karl was through with his last sentence, Bill Junior stood in his pew. He motioned for his parents to stand and when they did, all those they had invited stood with them. It was a good-looking support group for Bill Junior.

At least twenty five, maybe thirty people. Karl guessed.

As Bill Junior and his parent's scooted out of the pew and started down the aisle, Karl could see that the support group wasn't sure what to do.

"You all come with them," Karl said, as he motioned with his arm. At that, the rest of the congregation laughed approvingly, and the group moved down the isle and surrounded Bill Junior and his parents as they stood before Karl at the prayer rail.

"Bill junior, is this all you brought?" Karl asked, as he looked at the faces in front of him. The congregation laughed again, as Karl gave Bill Junior a hug.

After Karl re-arranged the group, so that the congregation could see Bill Junior and his parents, he shook hands with each person standing there and said; "Welcome" to each. Then Karl said to the congregation,

"What a privilege...for you and I this morning."

Looking first at his parents, then to Bill Junior, Karl said,

"Bill Junior do you renounce the forces of evil. If so say, 'I do.'"

Bill Junior said, "I do" loud enough for everyone in the Sanctuary to hear him, and the congregation laughed warmly, just a little.

"Do you profess Jesus Christ as your Lord and savior?" Karl asked.

"I profess Jesus Christ as my Lord and Savior," Bill Junior said loudly, just as they had rehearsed.

"Do you desire to be baptized into the Church of Jesus Christ?" Karl asked, knowing what was coming.

"I do I do I do," Bill Junior said loudly, and the congregation responded warmly. By now, most of the congregation knew Karl had changed the words and order for Baptism somewhat to fit the occasion, which was his prerogative.

"Do you promise to give to God some of your time, share your talent and give your tithe?"

174

"Yes I do!" Bill Junior said emphatically.

"Then Bill Bright Junior, kneel." Karl said. "And as he is kneeling, I'm going to ask the entire congregation to stand," Karl added.

Scott Thompson, standing beside Karl with the Processional Cross, reached over and took the top off of the Baptismal fount, just in time. Karl reached in with both hands cupped together and raised them, filled and overflowing with water. Karl rested them on top of Bill Junior's bowed head. As he slowly opened his hands the water poured out of them on to Bill Junior's head and flowed down over his face. Karl took his finger and while making the sign of the cross upon Bill Junior's forehead he said,

"Bill Bright Junior, I baptize you in the name of the Father and of the Son and of the Holy Spirit."

It was a moment Karl would never forget. Nor would Bill Junior's parents. Nor would the standing congregation. Bill Jr. stood up then, just as he and Karl had rehearsed. But what came next, they had not rehearsed.

Karl was preparing to say to the standing congregation, "Will you support Bill Junior in his walk of faith? If so raise your right hand and say, "I do"... but Karl never got a chance. First his parents, then the support group, began to hug Bill Junior. Then without asking, members of the congregation started coming forward to do the same thing. Within seconds the entire congregation was moving up the isles to embrace Bill Junior. Karl had never seen that happened before. He turned to Scott and said jokingly,

"I think we've lost control here Ron." Then it dawned on Karl, he didn't have to ask the question, this was a living answer.

Walking up the center aisle toward Bill Junior, Jerrey Walker pulled at Terry Habersham's coat. As Terry turned around Jerrey said,

"It's her!"

"It's who?" Terry asked.

"It's the girl and her brother and mother. Right there in front of Shelley. I can't believe it!"

The girl Jerrey had seen standing in line Thanksgiving Day. The girl he had eaten his second Thanksgiving dinner with. The girl he had chased down the street in his car. The girl he had spent two days looking for so he could protect her from, 'that man'. Who ever, 'that man' was. The girl and her little brother and her mother, were right there in front of them...safe, or were they?

Jerrey started looking around at those walking up the isle. He eyed those still standing in their pews. His eyes searched each face, looking for, 'the man.' When he reached Bill Junior, Jerrey gave him a quick hug and started to turn away, following Terry when Karl reached over and touched his arm.

"Ever find that family you were looking for? Karl asked.

"Ugh, maybe," Jerrey answered, embarrassed to be up front and speaking to the minister in front of all these people.

"Well, if you need any help, let me know," Karl added, as Jerrey nodded and walked away sheepishly.

As Jerrey followed Terry back up one of the side aisles, his eyes searched the congregation, looking desperately for 'the man'. He could be here! He could be, couldn't he?

Jerrey's mind was so confused over the entire experience, he hesitated to say anything to anyone anymore. While he walked and his eyes searched, his mind raced forward and bounced back to Thanksgiving Day. He had first thought the man was...but that was impossible, wasn't it? Jerrey thought in his confused state anything was possible.

"One thing was for sure," Jerrey thought, "this could be a dangerous or wonderful situation. If that stalker was here, then not only could that small family be in danger, but perhaps the entire congregation. Jerrey, yes, Jerrey might have to save the day. Might have to save the entire congregation. Surely the man wouldn't be that bold. He hadn't been in the past. He had been sneaky, there one minute and gone the next. That was his style. Not open and

bold but in the background. Out of sight or almost out of
sight. There but not there. Jerrey looked at every face.
Half way back to his pew Jerrey's eyes met Ashley's and as
they did she mouthed,
"Jerk"...and then smiled.
He wasn't a jerk. Was he? No, he wasn't. He was trying to
help them, to protect them, to look after them. She was
sitting with her Mother, brother and Shelley, for some
reason. If Shelley knew them, then Jerrey wouldn't have any
problem finding them later. He wouldn't alert them of the
possible danger, but he would continue to look. He assured
himself that this would be the correct move to make and so
he walked on with out stopping.
Then his eyes fell on Gwen Habersham who was looking at
him with a slight smile on her face.
"Wow!", Jerrey thought. "Wow!"
He had no idea that two people could talk to each other for
that long. Gwen and he had left the Habersham's last
evening after everyone else. They had both agreed, on the
Verandah, that they would love to see that movie. After
looking in the paper and discovering it was showing, they
had driven a half hour just to get to the theater. The movie
was as good as expected and they talked about it, and
everything else, while sitting at Bogey's Restaurant.
Jennifer, the owner, was still busy when they finally left at
three thirty in the morning. Jerrey had discovered, during
the evening, that Gwen Habersham was a delight to be with,
even though she said she was still shaken from that
afternoon's accident. She seemed remarkably calm to him,
but Jerrey knew in a few days it would all set in, and Gwen
would need even more rest. ...and as they left the restaurant,
while still sitting in the parking lot...when she leaned over
toward him and he knew she wanted him to kiss her...Wow!
Jerrey Walker knew that one kiss would be with him
forever. Like right now.
"Excuse me," a lady said to Jerrey as she stood behind him.
"Oh, I'm sorry," Jerrey said, as he stopped staring at Gwen
and moved on up the aisle.

As the last few were greeting Bill Junior and his parents, Scott leaned over to Karl and whispered,
"Maybe we'd better do the abbreviated version of communion today," and Karl nodded in agreement.
Karl loved the ritual normally used with Communion. Much of it had been handed down for hundreds of years. It allowed the people to participate in the ceremony and invited them to share the elements. But some times, an abbreviated version, as Karl and Scott had grown accustomed to calling it, was more appropriate, much shorter, and much simpler, and the correct way to celebrate and distribute the sacrament today.

When Betsy saw Mary with the tray of refreshments, she rose quietly to assist her. For while sitting in her rocking chair, Grandma had dozed off. The two women quietly arranged the glasses and pitcher on the table. Then Mary poured a fresh cup of coffee and placed it on the table, over to the side.
Standing on the Verandah, watching Grandma as she slept in the old rocker, the two women spoke softly to one another about days gone by: Mary's life as an adopted member of the family, and Betsy's life as a grandchild of the old lady. They both agreed on one thing above all, Grandma had always been just that...a lady.
They were both startled when Grandma spoke,
"Well, where have you been"? she said.
They turned to see her, still sitting in the rocker, staring straight ahead out into the open. The question wasn't directed to either of them. It was spoken as though directed to some one else.
"What do you mean, you've been right here?" Grandma asked.
"I've missed you so much," she added.
Both Mary and Betsy were frozen in place. Neither could move...for without saying a word, they realized whom Grandma was speaking to.
"Betsy", Mary said softly, as she put a napkin to her mouth,

"he's come back for her Betsey, he's come back for her."
Tears of excitement filled Betsy's eyes at the thought. *Was it true? Had Grandpa, come back for her, as Mary had just said. Was it possible?* Betsy thought, *Of course it's possible.*
"Of course," Grandma said, as she lifted her right hand. Both Mary and Betsy knew the old gesture. Grandma was putting her hand in the hand of an escort.
It had to be, Betsy thought. *Grandpa has come back for her.*
In a few seconds Grandma lowered her hand and head.
Standing motionless, looking at, the lady, Mary and Betsy knew Grandma had just left with the love of her life. She was going home with him. Now they would have eternity together.

Karl had spoken the words, broken the bread, raised the Chalice and prayed the appropriate prayer before commencing with the distribution of the Communion elements of bread and Wine. They were serving the second half of the congregation as, one by one, each came forward in a continuous line, when standing in front of Karl at the prayer rail was Jill and Tom Smith with their two children.
He blessed the two children by placing his hand on each of their heads and praying a short prayer. Then he turned to Tom and Jill, gave them the elements and smiled at each of them that knowing smile. And Karl knew. He had been watching the entire service. Jill and Tom with their two children had been accepted and included, without question, into the worship experience.
When the congregation had Shared the Peace of Jesus Christ, by each member greeting others around them, everyone around them had greeted them. He had caught a glimpse of their faces and they were filled with happiness. He knew the same would be true in the Church's other activities during the days and weeks to come. Tom, Jill and their children had found a home.
When Karl saw Ted and Evelyn Habersham easing toward him in line, soon to be in front of him, Karl looked for Ted's mother, but didn't see her. He guessed that perhaps she had

stayed home this morning, too tired to come after last evening's gathering.

God bless her. he thought. Everyone knew Grandma would be going home soon, maybe sooner than everyone expected.

When Ted was in front of Karl, Ron handed him the bread and Karl extended the chalice. After Ted dipped the bread into the wine...

Karl was given a thought.

It was not his thought. It came from outside of his mind. It was the type of thought Karl had learned to heed. The thought said;

His mother has come home.

Karl didn't hesitate. This time, he reached out his hand and made the sign of the cross on Ted's forehead and while doing so said,

"The blessings of God the Father almighty be upon you, now and forever more, amen."

Ted knew Karl seldom did that and when he did, it was for a very important reason. As he and Evelyn walked back to their pew, Ted thought he knew the reason. He knew when he had hugged his mother this morning it would be his last hug from her, this side of Heaven.

Bud Johnson was in line to be served right after the couple Karl was extending the chalice to. As Bud approached he held in his hand, up next to his chest, an airplane ticket so Karl could see it. It was a ticket, to Fairmont, West Virginia. Karl knew that Bud's wife was from there and in fact had taken the children there when she left Bud. Karl asked softly,

"Bud, is that a one way ticket or are you picking up and bringing back?" Bud smiled and said;

"I pray the latter Reverend, Pray for me." Karl handed him the chalice and instead of saying; "Take the blood of Christ shed for you," as he had everyone else, he said,

"May God heal the hurt and reunite your family Bud. Then Karl added, "Seen the paper this morning Bud?" Bud Johnson shook his head, no, as he moved away, but knew Karl had just told him something. Right after this worship service, Bud was going to buy a Sunday paper and find out what Karl had meant.

Bill Junior's eyes were fixed on the big man standing, up front, beside Karl and Scott. Unlike Karl and Scott, dressed in their black robes and bright stoles, the big man was dressed in a plain dark brown overcoat with a red scarf wrapped around his neck. Bill Junior could swear he had seen the big man before, but he couldn't remember where or when. Every once in a while, the big man would lean down and whisper something to Karl, and Karl would respond. ...and then...and then...and then it happened. The big man looked back, through the congregation, at Bill Junior, and smiled,...and Bill Junior remembered. Bill Junior's heart skipped a beat, as his soul overflowed.
"What are you smiling at, Bill Junior?" his Dad asked,.
"The big man standing up there beside Karl," Bill Junior replied.
"What big man? I don't see any big man Bill Junior," his Dad said.
"You don't see him? I do," Bill Jr. replied.

Jerrey Walker had been blessed beyond his wildest imagination that Thanksgiving weekend. It was true. He had seen Him, that big man, standing in line at the big church, with Katherine and her small family. Jerrey had spotted Him, walking with the people, on the streets of his small town. Jerrey would look for Him in the faces of everyone he came into contact with for the rest of his life, and Jerrey would see Him often.
Katherine had heard His voice, while standing in line at the big church, Thanksgiving Day. Jerrey Walker had been right, the same big man had been standing there with Katherine and her family, all along. He knows what it's like to stand in a line of one...all alone...all alone.
Earlier, during the week, Karl had been willing to miss his plans, for the sake of others. But Karl glanced at Him, heard his voice and gave the time, to He who gives us all time.

Karl, after all, didn't miss a hit, and now there He was, standing right beside Karl.

Jill and Tom sat at His table and shared coffee and donuts at the shelter, and yesterday evening, Gwen had seen the big man pointing in the right direction to save her life and she had obeyed. Her life on Earth would continue. Her descendants, and there would be thousands, would never know... but then again.

The small Sanctuary had been blessed before the sun rose that Sunday morning, for the Risen One had chosen to pray there that morning. Hell's fury, kept at bay, allowed all Heaven to break loose in worship. Hell's fury would try to rebound, that was for sure.

Grandpa's physical life had been stolen away. But his spirit had rejoiced in the knowledge that someday his prayer would be answered...and on that Sunday morning, the big man had told Grandpa to go ahead. Mary and Betsy were correct. Grandpa stepped back into time and space, and took his beloved home.

Now the big man stood beside Karl...and was shared with all who would accept the invitation. When He leaned down and whispered deep into Karl's spirit, Karl's heart pounded and his soul rejoiced in recognition. What Karl heard was:

"Tell them Karl, tell them...
Wherever they go. Whatever they do.
Whatever they go through. I am with
them.
Tell them, I will never leave them, Karl.
Quote, 'Lo I am with you always, even to
The end of he age?' Tell them Karl, tell
them."

At the end of the service, instead of his usual benediction, Karl said;

"Remember the words of our lord and savior Jesus Christ when he said;

"Lo I am with you always, even to the end of he age."

Remember, all this week, He is with you, go in peace."

182

Every one was shaking Scott and Karl's hands as they filed out of the church building. Ted and Evelyn politely turned down an invitation from the Walkers to join them and the Watts family for lunch. They wanted to get home and check on Grandma. Shelley wondered if Katherine, Ashley, and Sammy wanted to spend the afternoon at her home out in the suburbs. They had graciously accepted the invitation. Alice was going with the Walkers and said she would meet Karl at the restaurant. Bud Johnston had hurried to his car and was headed to the nearest newsstand. Terry Habersham was already half way home, shifting his sports car from one gear to the next and back again as he raced along the back roads to the ranch. He knew that his grandmother was probably okay, but he just wanted to make sure. He just wanted to see her again, and kid her about something, or talk with her, or...or...something...and Terry's eyes began to water again. Would she be okay when he got there?

"Oh, Grandma." He said out loud, as he pulled into the driveway.

As Karl walked back into the building to remove his robe and stole, he stepped into the quiet Sanctuary. Everyone was gone. For another week, the congregation had dispersed into the world.

This week they would experience the blessing of life, the greatest gift God had to give and, for those who would accept the invitation, even new life through Jesus Christ. Their lives this week would be tempered with challenge and they would be strengthened by the experience. But frustration would also barge in and breach the wall of peace. Hurt would try it's best to steal away their joy and sorry would shower down upon a few.

But, they would gather in this place again next week, to worship...and be renewed. Karl thought; "What would life be, without a place like this?" He knew the answer, even as he asked the question. Without God in a person's life, life is an empty shell and a shallow grave.

As Karl looked at the cross sitting up on the altar, he smiled...**not to himself**...and the thought came into his mind again,
"Lo I am with you always Karl, even to the end of the age."

YOU ARE NEVER ALONE!

Prologue

Out of respect, cars moving in the opposite direction pulled over to the side of the road and stopped, as the funeral procession approached and moved past them. After the hearse and limousines there were over thirty cars, each flying little flags with their headlights burning brightly. The procession moved slowly along the back country road from Karl's church toward the ranch.

It was the same road Terry had zoomed over just a couple days earlier, hurrying home from Sunday morning worship. In fact, Grandmothers passing had hit Terry the hardest. That was somewhat of a surprise to the rest of the family, but not to his mother Evelyn, or Mary. They had discussed often, while Terry was growing up, how smart he was, and how sensitive too. Now his grandmother wouldn't be around. He wouldn't hear her voice anymore, wouldn't see her face.

But she would be there rooting for him, and praying for him...both of them would be.